Acquitted by a jury of a crime he did not commit, Charles Ryder is nevertheless found guilty by his wife, his children and his superior in his job: or at any rate they do not find him wholly innocent as the twelve strangers had done.

Ryder is shocked and desperate. But the last accusation to be directed at him – something this time far more serious – causes him to fight back and then disappear. His disappearance is aided by villains with whom he is already in contact. His hidden life will lead him into the clutches of other villains, men far more sinister than Ryder can comprehend.

This is the story of a man's attempt to escape from a fearsome dilemma that is not of his own making: the twists and turns that are forced on him, the people with whom he makes and breaks friendships. It leads to a scene of blood-soaked violence, and a weird aftermath.

John Wainwright's reputation as a teller of stories is second to none. He is in fine form here as he recounts this ominous and gripping tale.

John Wainwright
Clouds of Guilt

MACMILLAN

ISBN: 0 333 38432 6

First published 1985 by
MACMILLAN LONDON LIMITED
London and Basingstoke
Associated companies in Auckland Dallas Delhi
Dublin Hong Kong Johannesburg Lagos Manzini
Melbourne Nairobi New York Singapore Tokyo
Washington and Zaria

Typeset in Great Britain by
BOOKWORM TYPESETTING
Manchester, England

Printed and Bound in Great Britain by
ANCHOR BRENDON LIMITED
Tiptree, Essex

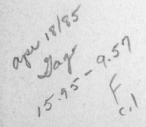

I walked from the Crown Court Leeds Town Hall in something of a daze. It must have shown in my expression, because occasional hurrying pedestrians paused long enough to stare before continuing on their way. Perhaps I staggered a little, was slightly unsteady in my walk. It wouldn't surprise me. Perhaps they thought I was drunk. I think I *felt* drunk. I certainly felt a little dizzy. Light-headed, to say the least.

I had cause to feel light-headed.

For some weeks I'd been shuttled between H.M. Prison at Armley and the lower court. Then the Leeds Crown Court and a dock shared by two accused villains. They'd faced a bank robbery charge. My charge had been one of conspiracy; conspiring with my dock-mates in that I had told them when the Haggthorpe branch of the Nat West had held enough money at the counter to make it worth their while to organise an armed robbery. Everybody had pleaded Not Guilty. I can only speak, with certainty, for myself. I *was* innocent. Unfortunately an ambitious detective chief inspector . . .

But no! I forced myself to be charitable.

He had not *manufactured* evidence. He had merely *slanted* it. From hours – literally hours! – of hard interrogation he'd hand-picked sentences and phrases, strung them together and constructed what amounted to an implied admission.

'You, of all people, knew when most money was available for theft?'

Dammit, of *course* I knew. As chief clerk I couldn't *not*

know. Come to that, and had they given it any thought, any of the tellers at the counters would have known.

'You were there on the public side of the counter when the thieves entered the bank?'

In God's name, why not? Coincidence. Nothing more. Part of my job was to interview customers and, having interviewed them, politeness demanded that I accompany them to the door of the bank. A dozen times a day I was on the public side of the counter. Common courtesy . . . and it was being screwed up to equate with guilt.

'When the thieves held the people up at gun-point, it was *you* who warned everybody – staff and customers alike – to do exactly what the raiders told them to do?'

So what? It was bank policy. More than that, it was *my* policy. One of the bastards had a sawn-off twelve-bore; the most devastating close-range weapon in the armoury. The other had a Mauser, 7.63mm; a ten-shot handgun with a muzzle-velocity capable of making the so-called bandit glass behind which the staff sheltered as useless as plaster-board. This I knew. No guesswork. I was a member of the Haggthorpe Rifle and Pistol Club. I savvied more about firearms than any other person in that bank. I *knew*. I acted accordingly.

Okay, I'll bend over backwards and give the man the benefit of doubt I can't even see. He was doing his job. He'd spent a small lifetime listening to smooth-talkers feeding him lies. But granting all that, the impression was that here was a copper who *wouldn't* be wrong . . . even when he was. Tell him the truth, and he boned it seeking meanings that weren't there. The police mind perhaps.

But what of the banker's mind?

We had different priorities. It was as simple as that. The copper couldn't drag his eyes from £200,000, whereas to me it was only *money*. Set alongside human life it was worthless . . . and it *was* being set alongside human life. Paper. Fancy paper – even expensive paper – but those stocking-masked

6

men would have killed for it. They would have killed and they had the means of killing. They weren't bluffing. The shotgun and the Mauser were both cocked and each had a finger on its trigger. I told him that, over and over again. That was my reason, and that was my only reason, but the fool wouldn't believe me.

'You prevented a member of the public – a customer – from getting to the door and noting the registration number of the getaway vehicle?'

Sweet whistling Christ! Of course I did. That Mauser terrified me. A supremely accurate long-distance handgun. The man – the customer – thought he was being a good citizen. A hero of some sort. He was no hero. He was a potential nut-case. A potential *dead* hero. I was trying to save the fool's life.

Those were a handful of the admissions I made. No not *admissions*. Explanations, and obvious explanations at that. But by the time this super-heated law enforcement officer had twisted those explanations around, and countered them by cunningly worded statements from staff and customers alike I was in trouble. 'Schnook' was my middle name. I was part of a gang of villains. The 'inside man', no less.

Nor had my two dock-companions inconvenienced themselves by throwing me a life-line. Understandable, of course. They had their own worries. They'd been far too busy saving their own skins to worry about the innocence of a mere bank employee.

Ergo, earlier that morning I'd come to accept the near-certainty of my conviction.

The barrister representing me was a wigged and gowned mouse. A non-entity, terrified of the judge, ingratiatingly polite to the Prosecution and tongue-tied in his closing speech to the jury. So I was jail fodder. Nothing surer. I'd made up my mind within the first hour. The hell of it was I was innocent . . . but I was still going inside.

In a manner of speaking, I became of age in that hour. I'd believed in British justice. Without waving flags or beating drums, I'd accepted the British bobby as the 'thin blue line' separating moderate decency from lunatic anarchy. The whole fairy tale. I'd been brought up to accept it, without question, and it had been very painful having the scales ripped from my eyes. Jerks were there among the polished oak. Goofballs who used big words to hide their own incompetence. And because of that, I was going inside for a long, long time.

The realisation scared the pants off me.

But I counted without my dock-companions.

They were villains. Thieves. Bank robbers, even. (The detective chief inspector had assured me of that; that the company he figured I kept was not from the top shelf. He'd even shown me the official form carrying their previous convictions in an attempt to 'break' me and on paper they were desperate characters.) But that they were *what* they were had been my salvation.

They knew their way through the jungle. They knew the people who earned their corn.

Their barrister had fought. Like an angry terrier on three occasions he'd barked the judge himself into a forensic knot-hole. Technicality after technicality. He'd threatened, bawled and bullied until the jury had had that vague, punch-drunk look of a class of numbskulls trying to understand the ins and outs of differential calculus. His cross-examination of Prosecution witnesses had been ruthless. Even the detective chief inspector had been made to look, if not a liar, at least more than slightly foolish, and had left the box with the sheen of sweat on his face. That barrister had won the case for his clients, and in that nobody can 'conspire' with himself, he'd also won *my* case by default. The judge had frowned open displeasure and had rounded on the jury for reaching a Not Guilty verdict . . . but what matter?

I was a free man. Three cheers for British justice, even if it creeps in through the back door.

Nevertheless, I walked away from Leeds Town Hall with dazed and drunken gait. It had been far too near for comfort.

It seemed sensible to settle my nerves before I returned home.

I chose a café almost opposite the town hall and ordered coffee. I opened the attaché case in which I carried my few belongings, took out pipe and pouch and settled down to watch the world through the café window. The traffic; motor-cycles weaving zig-zag patterns through the choke of cars and double-deckers. The pavements thick with people hurrying from where they'd come to where they were going; always hurrying, never strolling; never jelling that, wherever they were going, when they got there the chances were they'd have to wait. Lunacy on wheels. Lunacy on foot. A crazy world, and I was once more part of it.

I sipped coffee, smoked my pipe and silently philosophised.

All the correct chat about 'inner city deprivation'. There was also 'inner city madness', and I saw it that afternoon as my nerves slowly steadied. I saw it – maybe recognised it for the first time – because, contrary to expectations, I'd been slung back into it. It scared me a little. Okay, my cell-time had been very short . . . but long enough to drive a new realisation home. The rat-race was still there. The treadmill was still pounding around at its normal, impossible r.p.m. And as I saw things, I had some leeway to make up.

But not to worry. I was healthy and in my prime, and I was gradually getting used to the idea that I wasn't going to be wrongly convicted. I was free, white and slightly shop-soiled . . . so what the hell? One day I'd look back on these last few weeks, chalk them up to experience and maybe grin – albeit ruefully – at how easy it is to come unstuck.

The train back to Haggthorpe was the usual on-the-hour, stop-at-every station, BR clap-out. As grubby and as rattling as ever. Winding its way through the tatty outskirts of Leeds, then gradually into the open countryside. Stopping for the obligatory two minutes or so at each dormitory village, then grinding its way northwards towards the Dales and my destination.

The grass seemed greener than when I'd last seen it. The trees more shapely, more beautiful. The cottages and farms more cosy and picturesque. I'd once taken it too much for granted. I'd been lucky, without knowing how lucky I was. That once upon a time . . . but no more. Home, with all its faults, was still home.

From Haggthorpe I took a taxi. Angling slightly away from the Dales and towards the Vale of York. Flatter countryside and richer farmland. My own neck of the woods and the hamlet I'd figured on not seeing for some few years.

The paying of the taxi took almost the last of the cash I'd had with me at the time of my arrest and, as I walked the path to the door of the bungalow, I reminded myself to make out a cheque for more money next morning.

Okay, I admit it. I had a twinge of disappointment when Anne didn't open the door to greet me. She *must* have seen the taxi . . . but I kidded myself that her not showing herself was part of her distaste for exhibitionism. She'd be there. She'd be waiting beyond that door to greet me. To congratulate me.

The hell she was!

She was in the kitchen, bent forward and loading the dish-washer. She had her back to me and she didn't turn. I pushed the self-kidology to its limit, made believe she hadn't heard me arrive and gently spoke her name.

Without turning she said, 'I heard it on the local radio. You've got away with it after all.'

I tell you, friend. No man can count the watersheds in his life. Leaving school. The first long trousers. Passing examinations. The first job. Getting married. Making love to a woman for the first time. Scores. Hundreds. Some he forgets. Some he has to remember. Some he *never* forgets. They add up. The total is what he is; they combine to make him a complete – or incomplete – human being.

I wasn't unique. I was the same combination; the sum of what I'd made myself, plus what highlights in my life had made me.

I soaked in a hot, sudded bath and tried to make sense of my own personal balance sheet. The credits and the debits. The peaks, the troughs and the rest . . . the unimportant mush which had gone to make up the bulk of my life. I wasn't proud. On the other hand I wasn't ashamed.

I was the man who'd reacted to that remark by my wife. A normal reaction. *My* normal reaction.

I hadn't answered her, because I couldn't trust myself to answer her. Instead, I'd walked from the kitchen to the bedroom, deliberately sorted out clean underclothes, stripped and thrown the underclothes I'd been wearing into the basket, then walked to the bathroom and turned on the taps. Very stiff-legged and civilised. Very stone-faced and controlled.

I allowed the hot water to cleanse me as I forced myself to recall things.

That I had asked the police *not* to bring her to the police station. At that time it had all been a mistake, a spin-off from normal police enquiries, something which would, eventually, require a mild apology. I hadn't wanted to upset her.

That had set the pattern.

Later I'd sent word for her not to visit the prison. It was

11

still a mistake. It had gone further than I'd anticipated, but eventually it would be rectified . . . and this time there'd be one hell of an apology required. Meanwhile, save her the embarrassment of having to rub shoulders with the womenfolk of criminals. I'd even suggested she shouldn't visit the court. It might upset her. The newshounds might pester her. Anyway, when I arrived home I wanted her *there*, waiting.

Judas Christ! How wrong can a man be? How stupid?

She'd never intended visiting the police station, the prison or the court. Our policemen were wonderful. They didn't make mistakes. When they arrested a man he was guilty. Sod the court, sod the evidence, sod the verdict, sod what the man himself said. He was bent. The cops said so . . . therefore he *was* bent.

God, we were ruled by empty adages. Like potty-trained infants we obediently emptied our minds with the regularity of tots emptying bowels and bladders, then force-fed mock-wisdom into the empty spaces. 'The greatest legal system in the world'. 'Better ten guilty men go free than one innocent man be convicted'. That was the crap upon which she and her kind built lifelong beliefs. Carried to a conclusion it meant that no innocent man ever stood in a dock.

I towelled myself and was angry. Angry and outraged. Okay, I'd trained myself to control anger. Anger added nothing to discussion. That's what the banking profession taught. An argument centred around overdrafts and the like gets out of control if either anger or outrage eases a way in. So, keep cool. Keep the temper under firm control. The knack had spilled over into private life, and in the past it had helped to create a plateau of comfortable existence.

Great . . . but that plateau was crumbling fast.

I ran the electric razor over my cheeks, dressed in sports shirt and twill trousers and returned to the kitchen.

Anne had fixed a snack in the dining alcove. Paté and toast, followed by a light salad. Two places, and she joined

12

me at the table. She poured coffee, then sat down. Cool and quite composed. As if I'd just returned from the bank, not a Crown Court. Throughout the minor ritual neither of us spoke.

As I knifed paté onto a triangle of toast, I said, 'I take it you expected me to go to prison?'

'You're guilty, aren't you?'

Get it? That irritating woman's habit of answering a question by *asking* a question. Evasive and annoying. Dammit, why not say 'Yes.' Why not say 'No.' Why the hell lack the courage to *say* things?

And yet neither of us raised our voices. It remained a very civilised conversation. Terse, cool, but civilised . . . on the face of it. But no less hurtful, and based upon a false premise.

I said, 'Purely for the record, I was *not* guilty.'

'That being the verdict of the court.'

'That being the *truth*.'

'The police wouldn't agree.'

'Cops, too,' I growled.

'What?'

'*They* sometimes defecate and mistake it for thinking.'

'A typical remark,' she sneered.

'Typical,' I agreed. 'And true.'

I chewed the toast, swallowed, sipped coffee, then murmured, 'The police are human. Let's put it that way. They can make mistakes.'

'Do you expect me to believe that?'

'That they're human?'

'That they made a mistake?'

'Does it matter a tin-pot damn . . . what *you* believe?' As always, she was getting under my skin. 'They *did* make a mistake. I was – still am – innocent.'

'And you have a Crown Court verdict to prove it,' she mocked.

*   *   *

In retrospect . . .

Gentility. Respectability. That veneer they can wrap around you – wrap around a broken marriage – it can grow too thick and too hard. It can be like a tomb. It can prohibit all natural outbursts of emotion. The voice is never raised, the words are never vulgar; there is a smooth, icy politeness which can never be penetrated. Those two lunatic expressions 'the perfect lady' and 'the perfect gentleman' are yardsticks of moral cowardice. They equate with a reserve which can ruin any marriage.

I knew. I'd allowed it to ruin mine.

The situation was ridiculous. I was being called a criminal and a liar by my wife, and her expectation was that the most I'd do was smile sadly and gently shake my head. But this time . . . no! That veneer had been cracked. The man – *not* the 'gentleman' – had taken over, and the fury was there. Still under control, but ready to boil up and take over. Under the surface I raged and wanted to bring my balled fist down on the table and, if necessary, terrify her into believing the truth.

We continued our meal in silence, neither speaking nor looking at each other.

Part-way through the salad, I asked, 'Is Judy staying on late?'

'They're rehearsing *Twelfth Night*.'

'Oh?'

'She's been given one of the lead roles.'

'Good.' I popped a piece of hard-boiled egg into my mouth, swallowed it, then said, 'When's the performance?'

'A week tonight.'

'Do we have tickets?'

'One ticket.' There was a lot of meaning in those two words.

'One . . .'

'There seemed no point in buying two.'

'Can't you help it?' I growled.

'What?'

'Being a sanctimonious bitch.' It hit her, like a slap across the face. She didn't like it, and *I* didn't give a damn. I said, 'There should be some tickets left. I'll . . .'

'No!'

And now, it was her turn. In her own way she was fighting back. Very deliberately, she said, 'It's better if you don't go.'

'You have a reason for saying that of course.'

'It's better,' she repeated.

'That's not a reason. That's an opinion . . . a particularly lousy opinion.'

'It's reason enough.'

'Look . . .' My voice was low and hard. 'Judy's my daughter. She's appearing – indeed she has a main part – in her school's production of *Twelfth Night*. I'm proud of her. I'm damned if I'm going to . . .'

'She's not proud of you.'

'What the hell does that mean?'

'Charles.' She stopped eating while she spoke. 'Our children – Tim and Judy – have seen their father's name in the local newspaper far too many times recently.' She raised a hand an inch or two to silence me. 'You say you're innocent. I don't know. I don't *care*. What I *do* know is that the police don't make many mistakes. That's something everybody knows . . . including Judy, Tim, their school-mates and the parents of their schoolmates. If you go to that school play you'll embarrass your daughter. You'll embarrass me. You'll embarrass *everybody*.'

'There's a Crown Court verdict that . . .'

'The verdict isn't important. It is to you, perhaps, but not to anybody else.' Okay, she was being cruel, but maybe not deliberately cruel. I'd sense enough to realise that. She was a mother fighting for the happiness of her daughter . . . or so she thought. I realised that too, and reluctantly gave her what credit I could. 'That you were in a Crown Court dock. That you were charged with a serious crime of dishonesty. *That's* the important thing. *That's* what people remember. The rest doesn't count.'

'Judy,' I breathed.

'She's cried herself to sleep, night after night.'

'For God's sake, did she . . .' I was suddenly at a loss for words. 'Did she seriously think . . .'

'Charles, don't be stupid. Of course she "thought". She *still* thinks . . .'

'Like mother, like daughter.'

'If you care to put it that way.' Her tone matched my own. 'I can't keep you from that school play. But if you intend to go, don't buy another ticket. I shall not be with you. Nor will Judy be on stage. She'll have a convenient chill – a sore throat – something.'

'All neatly worked out.' I let the bitterness ride the remark.

'My children come first.'

'*Our* children . . . remember?'

'Charles, you're only their father. Any man can be a father. It doesn't take pain. It doesn't take love. All it takes is an erection and a willing woman.'

It is possible to weep without tears. All it needs is enough anger and enough heartbreak. The tears won't come, because the anger refuses them right of way. So they stay inside, and they burn. They scald. They feed the anger until reason itself seems to hang by a thread. Until madness seems to be within easy touching-distance.

I was learning things. Great truths. Basic emotions I hadn't known existed.

Learning . . . and hating.

Tim was out at his Yoga class.

Tim (three years older than Judy) was suddenly the rock upon which I sought to re-establish my shattered belief in

16

common decency.

Tim was one of the students at Haggthorpe Tech. Not quite university fodder, he'd been something of a disappointment to his mother. But not to me. From the start, I'd recognised the type. With Tim it was the old tortoise-and-hare stuff; let the high-flyers forge ahead, given time he'd overtake them when they'd burned themselves out. He had this knack, coupled with infinite patience: he insisted upon understanding everything about 'A' before he moved onto 'B'. Step at a time. No rush. He'd get there. One day he'd be the fine architect he dreamed of being . . . nothing surer.

For more than a year he'd been interested in Yoga. So like Tim. With other youths of a similar age it was football or nights out with the boys. Even more than a passing interest in girls. With Tim it was Yoga and (as in all things) he was deadly serious.

I parked the Volvo about ten yards from the entrance to the institute and waited. I almost prayed. Strange that, I'm not a praying man. When my religion is required on any document I dutifully write 'C of E', but that's something of a lie. Baptised – even confirmed – we were married in church, but like many of my kind I am at most a Christian agnostic . . . assuming such an animal exists. Nevertheless, I found myself whispering. 'Let him believe. Dear God, please let *him* believe.'

They came down the steps of the institute in a happy, close-knit crowd. Laughing (probably at the latest 'in' joke) but no pushing and no horse-play. Rowdyism wasn't Tim's style, consequently he didn't mix with rowdy types. He was a good son – a fine son: soon I'd know *how* fine.

I lowered the nearside window. He'd pass along the pavement to the bus stop. He'd pass the car and I would call his name.

Then what?

'Tim!'

My voice was throaty and not quite loud enough, so I tried again.

'Tim!'

He heard me the second time, peeled from the group, lowered his face to the open window and smiled. A real smile. Tim would never be ill-mannered, but at the same time he couldn't be false. It wasn't in him.

'Dad. I heard the news. The verdict . . .'

'I know. On the local radio.'

'. . . I was chuffed like crazy. Congratulations.'

The same reaction. The same reaction as Anne – almost the same words – but *not* the same reaction. I was listening for those subtleties of tone; how the words were phrased, but more importantly, where the emphasis was being put. I could detect nothing. Only pleasure. The pleasure of a son, happy that his father has come to the end of a trying experience.

As he climbed into the car I cleared my throat, and said, 'Not straight home, Tim, if you don't mind. Just a ride around. A talk. Not father-and-son stuff. Friends.'

'Sure.'

He nodded, and I knew he understood.

We drove in silence for all of ten minutes. From the centre of Haggthorpe; out along the Harrogate/Knaresborough road. Not for any particular reason. Nowhere specifically. Just to move around. A minor form of 'running away', perhaps. And if it was, who could blame me, and I wasn't running far.

The sodium street-lighting ended, and in the thickening dusk cars driven by fools came towards us with their headlights on dip. It didn't help. The glare seemed to push beyond my eyes and hit the base of my skull like a succession of laser flashes. Much more of it, and I was going to have the grandfather and grandmother of all headaches.

'A drink?'

'What?'

'Do you drink?' I asked. 'I'm sorry. I don't know.'

'I – er –' He hesitated.

'I'm not asking whether you get legless. Just . . . do you drink?'

'An occasional lager.'

'Good.' I nodded at the windscreen. 'We'll find somewhere.'

'Try a lay-by,' he suggested.

'*I* need a drink.'

'Sure. Okay.'

I pulled into the park of the next decent-looking inn. We found a snug; an empty room, which is what I was looking for. It was that betwixt-and-between time of the evening; customers would come later, but for the moment we had the privacy I sought. I bought half a lager for Tim and a single whisky, topped up with water, for myself. We settled at a corner table, tasted our drinks . . . then talked.

'Your mother thinks I got off,' I said quietly. Bluntly.

'So you did. The verdict came over the . . .'

'No.' I waved a hand. 'That I was lucky. That I was guilty, and got away with it.'

'Dad, the jury found you innocent. Nobody can . . .'

'Don't arse me around, son,' I interrupted gently.

'No . . . I'm not.'

'The jury doesn't count . . .'

'Dad, you can't dismiss the . . .'

'. . . *You* count. Your mother counts. *Judy* counts . . .'

'I can see that, but . . .'

'. . . Sod the jury. What *they* think isn't important.'

'No.' He shook his head. 'You can't dismiss them as easily as that. I know how you must feel, but . . .'

'Do *you* think I did it? That I helped armed men to rob a bank? My own bank? Do *you* think I was part of it and – to use your mother's words – "got away with it"?'

'Is it important?' he asked, solemnly.

'Dammit . . . yes! It's very important.'

'You were charged,' he said slowly. 'All along you've claimed to have had nothing to do with it.'

'Don't fence, son,' I pleaded. 'Say it, if it chokes you. Answer the question. Do you believe – have you *ever* believed – I was part of the bank robbery?'

'You want the truth?' He tasted the lager.

'That's why I met you. That's why we're here.'

'The police sometimes make mistakes . . .'

'Jesus Christ! If that's as far as . . .'

'Hear me out, Dad.' He was my son, but he spoke as an equal. That's what I'd asked for. That's what I was getting. 'They make mistakes. The legal system – this country's legal system – is good. Maybe the best in the world. But it's man-made, so it's not perfect. The trouble is . . .' A quick smile touched his lips. 'The media magnify the mistakes. A wrong conviction makes news. A thousand *right* convictions don't get mentioned. There's a slant . . . see? The mistakes. *Only* the mistakes. So, people like me tend to mistrust it. It's *all* mistakes.'

'I wasn't convicted,' I reminded him.

'It's the *mistakes* that make the news, Dad. Ergo, almost every verdict is one more mistake.'

'That's sheer crap,' I growled.

'Okay. Add what some silly judge has to say, if *he* doesn't believe in the verdict.'

'That's a hell of a stupid argument, Tim.'

'And other things, of course.'

'Such as what?'

'The various civil rights people. They go off at half cock very often. Without meaning to, they make the whole system suspect . . .'

'A handful of lunatics who . . .'

'Very *important* lunatics. They hand-pick their cases. They know the system *can* go wrong, even though it's a rare occurrence. But they make it sound as if it's *never* right. As if it's *always* wrong.'

'I was innocent,' I breathed.

'Sure, but if the system's consistently wrong?'

'Dammit, I *was* innocent.'

'Sure.' He tasted his lager. 'I'm just trying to make you see how mother feels.'

'I *know* how she feels. She's left me in no doubt.'

'Okay . . . *why* she feels that way.'

'I was *innocent*,' I breathed wearily.

'Sure.' He tasted the lager again.

'You don't believe me?'

'I believe in British justice.'

'Damn British justice! It's what *you* think that matters.'

'I believe in British justice, therefore I believe you're innocent. I don't *know* – only *you* know – but I have faith, therefore I believe.' He leaned fractionally nearer across the table. 'Dad, that's as far as I can go. As far as anybody can go. As far as the jury could go.'

'But always room for doubt,' I said bitterly. 'That bloody "reasonable doubt", eh? Leave the door slightly ajar, son. Don't commit yourself. Even for your own father.'

He looked sad, but remained silent. In retrospect, I don't blame him. Being what he was – who he was – he couldn't lie. Not even to give comfort. Maybe I admired his honesty. On the other hand, maybe I momentarily hated him for it. The only thing I know for certain is that I felt real desperation as we sat in silence.

'Judy?' I whispered, at last.

'She's cried a lot,' he said gently.

'Couldn't somebody *tell* her?' I asked, plaintively.

'Tell her what? That you'd been wrongly charged? Later, maybe, that you'd been wrongly convicted? She wouldn't have believed it. This family, Dad – you taught us – we don't tell lies.'

'It wouldn't have been a lie.'

'It *could* have been,' he countered quietly.

'Tim, don't you know me?' I groaned. 'Could you, for one moment . . .'

'The police thought so. You have to remember that. They were sure, otherwise they wouldn't have stood you in the dock.'

'The hell with what the police thought . . .'

'The magistrates thought so. They committed you to the Crown Court. It's not that easy. Who does know . . .?'

'*I* know.'

'. . . Judy's a very impressionable kid. You've been to prison. You can't deny that. You've been to prison, on remand. It all adds up.'

'To . . . guilt?' The damn word almost choked me.

'No. To a *possibility*.'

I fought the tide of rage. The rise of impotent fury. I tilted my head back and gulped in deep breaths in an attempt to keep control of myself.

Tim waited. I think he knew. I'm sure he knew. I credit him with knowing. Not understanding, but knowing . . . at least a little. He waited until I'd composed myself and, all the time, he looked unhappy. Not unsure. At his age – at Judy's age – kids are so damn sure. So sure . . . therefore so unhappy.

I sipped whisky and water before I spoke.

In as steady a voice as I could make it, I said, 'Tim, when I met you this evening – when you climbed into the car – you seemed pleased to see me. Pleasant. Happy. I – y'know – a man involved in a bank robbery. That's what it boils down to. So it seems. All right, your father . . . but that doesn't explain things. Not to me. To you, maybe, not to me. At the very least, a man *possibly* involved in the armed robbery of a bank. That's what you think. You, your mother, Judy . . . that's the size of it.' I paused, and he waited. I continued, 'Tim, I don't get it. It's beyond me. That you, my son, for whom I have great admiration – whom I love – can greet a possible bank robber as a friend.

Forget the "father" bit. That's what you did. No hesitation. No embarrassment. As if nothing had happened. And yet you refuse to accept my innocence, other than with qualifications. It's beyond me. I don't understand.'

He nodded, slowly, and smiled. It was almost a condescending smile. Almost. Not quite. It lacked the subtle arrogance of condescension. Rather, resignation with a touch of distress.

He murmured, 'Dad, if I said "Yama", would you understand?'

'No,' I admitted. 'I wouldn't know what the hell you were talking about.'

'The first level of attainment in Yoga.'

'Uhu.'

'There are eight levels. Far more than I'll ever reach. The first is Yama.'

'Big deal. And that explains things?'

'Dad, listen . . .'

'Lotus positions. All that guff?'

'No! It's *not* guff.' I'd hit him where it was raw. Great. Maybe somebody needed hitting where it was raw. He continued in a quieter tone, 'The lotus position is part of every level. We're not talking about gimmicks, Dad. It isn't glorified keep-fit. It's serious. The real thing. And I'm just about at Yama.'

'That first level?'

He nodded.

'Some sort of religion?'

'Call it a near-religious experience.'

'Okay,' I sighed. 'A near-religious experience. What does that mean?'

'I don't think you'd understand.'

'Too dumb, is that it?'

'You know that's not it.'

'Okay. Try me.'

He paused, as if to gather his thoughts, then said, 'A

control of the emotions, see? Absolute control. No envy. No selfishness. Charity, the basis of all things. The basis of all thought. It's a purely mental state. Very necessary. You don't hate any more. You don't criticise any more. You simply *accept*.

'Like a blasted zombie,' I growled.

'Dad, you won't even try to . . .'

'I'm sorry. Go on. I'm listening. I'll try to understand.'

'Well, that's it.' His smile was without rancour. 'Not a bit like a zombie. Quite the opposite. Yama represents positive control. Positive acceptance. A positive refusal to criticise. A positive refusal to hate.'

'It must be difficult.'

I softened my tone. I was a little ashamed at my reaction to what he'd said. I didn't want to hurt him. At that moment I could see no badness in him. Only a young man trying to come to terms with life in his own non-aggressive way.

I repeated, 'It must be very difficult.'

'It comes,' he said mildly. 'With practice – with application – it gets easier. It makes for tranquillity.' He tasted his lager, then spoiled everything by continuing, 'It wouldn't have made a scrap of difference. If, in fact, you are guilty – if, instead of being acquitted, you'd gone to prison – if you'd just come from prison after serving your time. It wouldn't have made any difference. The greeting would have been the same. I don't sit in judgement, Dad. Yama makes everything . . .'

'Everything sweet and charming,' I sneered. 'The world's fine and dandy . . . so don't piss on the roses.'

'Dad, you asked me to . . .'

'If?' I interrupted savagely. I downed the whisky, and ground out, 'If! *If*! IF! Why in hell's name is there always an "if" in the way? Why is there always doubt? My own damn family. Why can't they *believe*? Just that? Why do they disbelieve, or qualify what belief they have with crazy, pseudo-religious garbage? Why not, "You didn't do it. We *know* you didn't do it"? Dammit, that's not asking too much.'

'Oh yes.' He nodded, solemnly.

'What?'

'It's asking too much.'

'For Christ's sake . . .'

'We don't "know" . . . not the way you mean. Only you know.'

'Finish your lager.' Suddenly, he was a stranger. A not very nice stranger. A mealy-mouthed young pup who had doubts about his father's honesty, and hadn't the guts to voice those doubts. I stood up from the table, and said, 'We've talked long enough. Let's get home. Your mother might be worrying about where you are.'

I spent the night in the guest bedroom. That night and every other night. But that night was the first night. It was no hardship, and it was my own choice. Anne made no objection and asked no questions. The wry thought struck me that, on occasions, both Anne and I could control our emotions enough to get by . . . and without Yoga.

Nevertheless that evening – the evening of the return of the Prodigal Son! – was not a roaring success. Tim went straight to his room, and that was the last I saw of him that day. Judy came in from her rehearsal, saw me in the armchair, gulped, then she too ran to her bedroom.

Almost conversationally, Anne said, 'She'll probably cry herself to sleep.'

'Puberty,' I grunted. I didn't even look up from the book I was reading.

Later, when I'd finished the chapter, I said, 'You can attend the school play without embarrassment. I won't be there.'

'A wise decision.'

'Yeah . . . I'm learning wisdom at breakneck speed.'

If any other exchange took place between us I can't remember it.

Later, I read in bed for a short time, until I realised the words were reaching no farther than my eyes. I'd read at least two pages, and it hadn't registered. I placed the open book on the bedside table, linked my fingers at the back of my neck and tried not to feel sorry for myself as I assessed this lunatic situation. The cause . . . and its effect.

I reached certain firm conclusions.

I'd faced the charge of being the 'inside man' in the armed robbery of £200,000 from the Haggthorpe branch of the Nat West. I'd escaped conviction by the skin of my teeth; not because of the efforts of my own bungling barrister, but as a by-product of the skill of a barrister representing two villains sharing the dock with me. As an innocent man, I'd spent some weeks in prison on remand; again, the result of a solicitor at the lower court who was on a par with the barrister at the Crown Court. Had I searched the length and breadth of the UK I might never have found a more useless duo of forensic clowns, but because lawyers *make* the law, I had no redress . . . I'd had a choice and I'd chosen badly.

Okay, eventually, the law had performed its proper function. Very creakingly, very slowly and with the minimum of efficiency, it had ground into gear sufficiently well to return freedom to an innocent man. On the face of it I should have been aggrieved, but at least satisfied.

I was not.

I was being treated as a criminal. And by my own family! As far as they were concerned, I *was* a criminal. The verdict meant damn-all. My own protestations meant less. I'd dodged a way around the legal system and ducked my due deserts.

At first, I had not understood it. It had hurt and outraged me. It *still* hurt and outraged me, but on reflection I realised I'd been cunningly brainwashed. By the media

26

. . . who else? By so-called television 'documentaries'. The criminal – a real bent bastard – returns home having spent years behind bars. He was as guilty as sin, and makes no denial of that fact. He doesn't even promise to behave himself in future. But for the moment he's paid the price demanded by society, therefore hugs and kisses all round. Parties to celebrate his release into the world. He's back . . . and everybody adores him.

Not so with me, *and I was innocent*.

It was a puzzle, and it was a puzzle I cracked as I lay in bed cogitating. I traced the missing element.

Love.

This family of mine had no love. It was that simple. Somewhere, somehow, 'respectability' had smothered all affection.

I don't mean the slobbering, tall-dark-and-handsome garbage. Nor do I mean the never-ending fornication which, to certain writers and film-makers, forms the basis of modern, with-it marriages. I mean basic, happy-to-be-with-you love. Dammit, I could live without *them* and they could live without *me*. It hurt like the very devil, but having found the truth I faced it.

Next question: whose fault?

That question hadn't a simple answer.

I'd loved Anne when I'd married her. Obviously. At that moment I couldn't fathom out what had *made* me love her – whether I'd changed, she'd changed or we'd both changed – but I had to have a starting point and, short of accepting that I'd once been a flaming idiot, that seemed as good a starting point as any. Okay, it had been *my* kind of love. The only love of which I'd ever been capable. Nothing fiery. Nothing all-absorbing. Nothing too demanding of either of us. But as I remembered, her love for me had been built on a similar basis. We'd been 'comfortable' – even happy – in each other's company. Our likes and dislikes had tallied. Nevertheless – and make no mistake about it –

genuine love . . . as we both understood that word.

Now we hadn't even that. Nor, it would seem, had our children. Somehow we'd pulled off a vanishing trick; a hundred per cent Merlin masterpiece.

The realisation nagged at my mind. It nagged because I was honest enough to accept the fact that I, too, had lost something. Whatever I'd once had. Love, to use a ready word. An abstract. Something which couldn't be handled or sensibly estimated. Whatever it was, it couldn't be banked, it gave no interest, nobody could invest it, it didn't represent an overdraft, it wasn't even collateral . . . whatever it was. It wasn't of the banking world, therefore to me it was beyond the reach of easy understanding. Nevertheless, it had a value and I was the poorer for having lost it.

I was reminded of one of those Russian dolls; a doll within the hollow interior of another doll and which, in turn, is hollowed out and contains a yet smaller doll. Sometimes as many as eight – even ten – dolls, each progressively smaller and hidden inside slightly larger companions. But at the centre is a *solid* doll. Less than thimble-sized, yet the core around which the hollow dolls are built.

Like the Ryder family, but somehow, somewhere we'd lost that all-important solid doll. A series of hollow shells – progressively less important façades of approval – but inside . . . nothing. No real feeling. No damn-your-eyes adoration.

The realisation made for sorrow and some bitterness, but I'd had a long and tiring day. I switched off the light and went to sleep.

Masters said, 'You realise we can't of course,' and had the grace to look uncomfortable as he spoke.

I stared across the desk at him, then said, 'I realise you *won't* . . . which isn't the same thing.'

'The decision isn't mine, Charles,' he sighed.

'And if I refuse?'

'We think you have enough sense not to make even more trouble for yourself.'

Trouble? No . . . *more* trouble? The arrogance took my breath away. Somewhat academically I wondered whether this man, Arnold Masters, knew the meaning of the word. He could have been the matrix used for every successful bank manager. A big man; big enough to dominate, but not big enough to intimidate. Well-built. Muscular and well-padded without being fat. Well dressed – indeed immaculately dressed – but not flashy and not old-fashioned. Clerical grey suited him; it went with the hair and set off the white shirt and darker grey tie. A clean-looking man. Clean, bright and (when he was his usual self) slightly friendly. Not gushing, but ready to listen. Ready to listen, but not necessarily to believe. In fairness, the right man in the right place.

But *trouble*?

I'd worked with him, and alongside him, for too many years. I knew his background. His life had been as smooth as plate glass, and he'd glided from post to post, always in an upward direction, without the inconvenience of a lost wink of sleep. That's how much he knew about trouble.

'I've done nothing wrong,' I argued gently.

'We accept that, of course. The court found you . . .'

'Not the court. Damn the court. Me! I, personally, have done nothing wrong.'

He nodded. It could have been a nod of agreement. Equally, it could have been the nod of a man who's grasped the gist of an argument, without subscribing to that argument. It was a very professional nod. A very safe nod.

'What I did,' I continued, 'I did in the interest of the bank. In the interest of customer safety.'

'Forgive me, Charles.' He leaned back in the desk chair and smiled. 'You're arguing with the wrong man. It's out of

29

my hands.'

'Policy from on high?' I returned the smile, and mine was as false as his.

'Exactly.'

'My resignation?'

'With three month's severance pay.'

'Tell me,' I asked gently, 'Why am I resigning?'

'Caesar's wife,' he murmured, with equal gentleness.

'That's no answer.'

'The bank is Caesar, Charles.'

'Ah!' I nodded slowly. 'The bank.'

'We handle our customers' money. We must not only be honest. We must be *obviously* honest. No doubt. Not even the hint of a doubt.'

'And I represent that "hint"?'

'Nothing personal, Charles.'

Rather slowly and very distinctly, I said, 'Masters, don't be such a pompous prick.' Then, when his jaw almost dropped, I continued, 'If I sign that bloody resignation I can say that. I don't have to touch my forelock any more. Not to you. Not to your precious bank, and not to the smooth-talking prats who tell *you* what to do. I know. It's all very gentlemanly, isn't it? All very civilised? The hell it is . . . and we both know it.

'This glorified money-box is the all-important reason for it all. Not people. Not employees. A court – the findings of a jury – is nothing by comparison. I *might* have. I just might! It needs no more than that. Courts have been wrong. Juries have returned wrong verdicts. But, oh my Christ, the bank must *always* be right. Three cheers for the bank. Stand up and salute the bank.

'Acne-faced students have to feel safe that they can ask for outrageous overdraft facilities. Old ladies, with more money than sense, mustn't be put off. They have to feel sure that their savings aren't being frittered away by dubious characters employed by this fiscal fantasia. Oh, not just this bank. *All* banks. Every blasted bank that ever issued a cheque book.'

I paused, then ended, 'I'll sign your infernal resignation, Masters. What choice have I? I'll sign it. I'll take the severance money. The *conscience* money. But between these four, very expensive walls, I'm beginning to wish I *had* been part of that damned robbery. I couldn't have been *worse* off, and I might even have been a rich man.'

And now I hadn't a job. Nor had I any great prospect of finding another job. My profession was banking and no other bank was going to employ me. They'd ask where I'd previously worked and telephone Masters. Thereafter, smiles all round, a polite handshake and, in that oblique terminology beloved of the breed, leave me in no doubt that they were not prepared to pick up the unwanted droppings from the Haggthorpe branch of the Nat West.

I found a vacant bench on the Common. Somewhere to sit and ponder. Somewhere to contemplate the future. Somewhere to feel a little sorry for myself, and feel disgust at the world in general and, specifically, at the make-believe way of life we call civilisation.

Take Haggthorpe. Population around the 150,000 mark and, in the old days, a municipal borough. No industry worthy of the name, it modelled itself on the spa town of Harrogate. It was a very second-best model. Even the Common was Haggthorpe's answer to Harrogate's Stray. It lacked a conference centre, its 'spa baths' was a sick joke in bad taste, but it was within easy distance of the real thing and it had hotels and it had wealth. A strangely Victorian wealth. A wealth typified by massive, stone-built houses (most of them converted into flats or offices) and a distinct nose-in-the-air attitude of its inhabitants.

I'd been privy to the financial status of many of those inhabitants for more than seven years, and could vouch for

31

the fact that most of the fur coats had been paid for, that the sprinkling of jewellery shops carried (and sold) stock rarely available outside London and that, although the £200,000 robbery had hogged the local headlines, the fact remained that·more than a few of the bank's customers could have signed a cheque covering that amount and still have enough left to keep them in comfort for the rest of their lives.

A 'money' town. A place of rich widows, flowered hats and a premium of bored and ailing husbands. A town of gentlemen's clubs where directors, managers and the like assembled and paid through the nose to be pampered and coddled as the whim took them.

A two-tier society. Those who served and those who demanded service. And the gap between was as wide as the Grand Canyon. A gap that couldn't be bridged in one lifetime. Forget football pools. Forget all the get-rich-quick schemes. That much-abused word millionaire was just that . . . a much-abused word. They weren't at every street corner, and the ones who lived at Haggthorpe rarely mentioned it. They'd inherited wealth – often added to it – and took it as much for granted as the water which flowed when they turned a tap. They were . . .

'We were bloody lucky.'

The remark imposed itself on my thoughts. I turned my head and for the first time realised I'd been joined on the bench. At first I recognised him only as somebody I *should* know . . . then I recognised him. Wilkinson. One of the men with whom I'd shared the dock.

I stared for a moment at a loss for words. Dammit, what do you say to a stranger who, because he's accompanied you on a short journey through hell, is no longer a *complete* stranger?

He smiled, then amplified the remark to, '*You* were very bloody lucky.'

I found myself returning the smile, and saying, 'Thanks

to your barrister.'

'A right flaming stumer you picked.' The smile expanded into a quiet chuckle.

'My solicitor,' I murmured.

'Eh?'

'*He* chose him.'

'Don't pay the bloody bill.' Then very solemnly, 'I reckon we owe you an apology, mate.'

'Somebody does,' I agreed quietly.

'We didn't name you.'

'Of course not.'

'We didn't name *anybody* . . . not even each other.'

'Not even the driver,' I said.

'Nobody.' He fished in a pocket, produced what looked to be a gold case, snapped it open and offered me a cheroot. As I took one, he added, 'Rules of the game.'

'Some game,' I sighed.

As he held the flame of the lighter I tried for a quick assessment. Hard as nails. Tough as teak. But no Bill Sikes type. Moderately well-dressed. North Country vowels and blunt to the point of rudeness, but no mug. In no way unsettled. Quite cheerful, in fact. About the same age as myself, but stocky and with an aggressive jut to the jaw. Pass him on any pavement and the expression 'middle executive type' might spring to mind.

He snapped the lighter out, returned lighter and case to his pocket, removed the cheroot from his mouth, blew smoke, then quite calmly said, 'We were as guilty as hell, of course.'

'A safe enough admission . . . *now*.'

'Look – what is it? – Ryder?'

'Charles Ryder.'

'Mind if I call you Charles?'

'Feel free.'

'Thanks. My name's William – Bill to my friends, remember?'

33

I nodded.

'It's like this, Charles. The law's a bloody ass. That's been said before. But it's driven by bloody donkeys. Coppers – up to and including superintendents – I wouldn't pay 'em in Smarties. They're all pantomime characters. Opening notebooks, licking pencils, swaying about on their size twelves. Crime pays, mate . . . *they* make sure of that.'

'Does it?' I asked, politely.

'What?'

'Pay? Crime?'

'*I* live pretty good.'

'Certainly *honesty* doesn't pay,' I said sadly.

He raised thick, questioning eyebrows. I'd tried to keep self-pity from my tone, but I suppose a certain amount of disgust tinted the words.

'I've been required to resign.' I made it a flat statement, without emotion.

'The hell you have!'

'The hell I *have*,' I assured him.

'Sodding coppers.' He frowned annoyance.

'Not the police . . .'

'Don't you believe it, mate. They'll have been putting it around.'

'Wilkinson . . .'

'Bill.'

'Bill.' I smiled. 'I've stood in a Crown Court dock charged with serious dishonesty. That's all it needs. Banks don't share your opinion of policemen.'

'They live in their own bloody world,' he grunted.

'Maybe. It's a world I'm no part of.'

'That's a crying shame.'

'Isn't it, though?'

'Look . . .' He held the cheroot between his teeth while he fished around in an inside pocket. He produced a letter, removed it from its envelope, then took a ballpoint and scribbled a telephone number under the address. 'Keep in touch. Before you reach the dole queue, contact me.'

'That's not . . .'

'Don't bloody argue. We owe you more than an apology.'

'Look, I'm not . . .'

'What's *your* address?'

'There's no need to . . .'

'Don't be a mug, Charles.'

I gave him what he'd asked for and he scrawled it on the letter, then he stood up, grinned, wished me cheerio and walked away.

Honour among thieves, perhaps? If not honour, at least understanding. True, he was one of the three people who *knew* I was innocent. He didn't need a jury to tell him.

The thought struck me. He could have opened his mouth before the trial. That would have been a *real* help. Maybe that, too, was one of the 'rules of the game'.

On the other hand, maybe he had and nobody had believed him. That, too, was a possibility.

I was beginning to share his opinion of policemen. One policeman in particular. A certain detective chief inspector.

I arrived home at my usual time. It had been a dreary, boring day but I'd decided not to mention my enforced 'retirement'. It would have merely reinforced an already-held belief in my guilt. I could leave and return home as if still employed at the bank. They'd never know; they never telephoned me at work and, when they used the bank, they never went beyond the counter.

I wasn't a rich man, but my means were moderate and I'd enough fat to live on for a few weeks. Until I'd sorted things out and reached decisions.

Nevertheless, I tried to be honest with myself. I wasn't going to find work carrying the salary I'd been earning. Indeed, I'd be lucky to find reasonable employment anywhere. Outside a bank I was unskilled labour and I'd never again work *inside* a bank.

There was also a little thing referred to in polite circles as marital problems.

Anne was my wife. I had a certificate to prove it . . . but not much else. She fed me, but with ill-grace and no imagination. She rarely spoke to me. She certainly didn't share my bed, or even my bedroom. In her eyes I was a necessary pariah and presumably would remain so. During those first few days there wasn't so much as a hint of softening up.

She was also poisoning my children against me. When I was at home Judy pointedly hurried through any room I happened to be in. Tim nodded cool greeting when politeness demanded, but wanted no conversation.

Once I snarled, 'What is this? Another aspect of this Yoga thing?' but he smiled and didn't answer.

I spent much of those first days in the public library. It was dry, reasonably quiet and the armchairs were an improvement on benches round the Common.

On the fifth day of my enforced leisure the envelope arrived in the first post. It was addressed to me and marked Private and Confidential. I took it with me and opened it in the privacy of the library. Inside was a cheque for £5,000, made out in my name and signed *W. Wilkinson*.

I remembered his words. 'We owe you more than an apology.'

Had Anne shown any sign of even half-believing; had she not been so utterly convinced that I *was* a criminal; had she even encouraged Judy and Tim to ask questions and make up their own minds . . .

Anybody can be monumentally wise after the event, but I think Anne's attitude nudged me over the demarcation line. All my life so damned honest. So careful. So infernally

36

righteous. And yet the only kindness shown to me since my acquittal had come from a self-confessed villain. He *knew* I was innocent. Knew it with the certainty of his own guilt. Knew it, and understood.

Forty-two is a strange age. You aren't yet old – maybe not even middle-aged – but you're no longer young. The latest fads tend to irritate. The realisation that mortality is the only real certainty is beginning to dawn. Ideas and ideals are fixed. Opinions have been formulated. Likes and dislikes have been decided.

It almost needs dynamite to shift you.

Especially with a man like me. Middle-class, clean-living and not given to experimenting with anything new. And, above all else, drilled since early youth to a way of life and a personal discipline.

Strange emotions were pushing their way to the surface. I couldn't hold them; either they were becoming stronger or my control over them was becoming weaker. I stared at the cheque and felt a pricking behind my eyes. This man – this Wilkinson – owed me nothing. Nothing! Not even an apology. I'd stood in the dock with him, but *he* hadn't put me there. Not Wilkinson. The police had put me there. The damn police.

Nevertheless, *he* wanted to make amends.

For what?

I fished his envelope from my pocket, left the library and walked to the nearest telephone kiosk.

I recognised his voice, pressed the coin into the slot and introduced myself.

'Charles. Good to hear from you.'

I took a fairly deep breath, then said, 'I got your cheque.'

'Great.'

'I can't possibly accept it.'

'Why the hell not?' He sounded genuinely surprised.

'It's not . . .' I didn't want to hurt the man, but it had to be said. 'It isn't your money.'

'It *is*,' he countered.

'What I mean is . . .'

'What you mean is you have a conscience. That's what you mean.'

'I suppose so,' I muttered.

'A bloody expensive luxury.'

'Damn it all, Wilkinson. If I . . .'

'Bill.'

'All right, Bill. If I accept this money I'll be . . .'

'If you don't accept it, you'll be a mug. It's not nicked.' The chuckle was soft and fat. 'Leeds Crown Court says so.'

'I don't give a damn about Leeds Crown Court.'

'You should. The other verdict, and *it* wouldn't have lost sleep.'

'That's not the point.'

'Charles, cash that bloody cheque.' It was almost an order. 'Cash it. Give the money to some charity, if that's what you want. If you're so well heeled.'

'I'm not,' I admitted quietly.

'So cash it, and don't argue.' There was a pause, then, 'Where are you eating?'

'I – er – I don't know. I haven't . . .'

'Know Ripon?'

'Yes, fairly well.'

'Spa Hotel?'

'That's the one on the Pateley Bridge Road?'

'That's the one.'

'I know it,' I said.

'They serve great lunches, Charles. Why don't we eat together?'

I found myself asking, 'What time?'

'One? A snifter first, then food. But cash the cheque first. No arsing around, Charles. If you don't I'll be hurt.'

'Thanks,' I breathed.

'No need. See you in Ripon at one.'

I paid in the cheque. I opened a new account, in my own

38

name and not, as was the case up to that moment, a joint account with Anne. Nor did I use the Nat West. That would have been foolish. Instead I used another high street bank.

I admit to a few moments of doubt. Of worry and apprehension. £5,000 out of the blue *buys* worry, doubt and apprehension. It really *wasn't* my money, argued which and every other way. Nor, come to that, was it Wilkinson's money.

So, the big question: whose money *was* it?

Not the bank's. No bank, of itself, owns money. Banks *handle* money. Save it, invest it, lend it, do mystical multiplication tricks with it . . . but they never *own* money. Banks – all the high street banks – are market places whose sole commodity is cash. In effect, they sell it and buy it. They pass it back and forth. They use it. Juggle it around. Turn it into figures on a computer sheet . . . then skim off a careful percentage in order to keep the market place in smooth and comfortable being.

I *know*. I've been in banking too long to have illusions. No high street bank handles a penny of its own cash.

Therefore, whose money? To whom could I hold out the cheque and say, 'Here. This is yours.'?

That conscience Wilkinson had scorned worked on over-drive. Had I been able to find a way through that fiscal forest I might have handed that cheque to somebody with more right to it than myself. But I couldn't figure a way of finding anybody . . . so I cashed it and opened a new account.

Then at just before twelve-thirty I climbed into the Volvo and headed for Ripon.

Ripon. The smallest cathedral city in the world. Time was it was part of the West Riding of Yorkshire . . . until some kooky-brained yuck in Whitehall decided a whole contained four thirds. Ridings. Since Norman William carved up the kingdom and before, the White Rose county had been Riding-divided; North, West, East Ridings. Now there are *four* divisions. North, West, South and Humberside. God in His glorious Heaven knows why. At a guess to give some clown a flyer at immortality.

Haggthorpe, Harrogate, Ripon, Knaresborough. They were once – and not too long ago – west. They'd been west for centuries. Now they're north . . . by order of kooky-brained yucks.

I could take Ripon or pass it by without heartbreak. A market square, complete with 'wakeman' who blows a fool of himself for the benefit of visitors every day. Some shops and supermarkets; banks and building societies; offices and hostelries. A typical market town, but with some very up-market hotels. Egon Ronay, AA-starred and RAC-starred, and none better than The Spa Hotel.

Tucked away and hidden from view to people moving no farther than the square, The Spa is known to those who matter. The discerning, professional-class citizens of Ripon, those from around who have the sense to recognise a good meal and a good drink, and visitors who have discovered The Spa in the past and have no wish to experiment elsewhere.

Its lounges are lush and deep-piled. Armchaired and open-fired. Deep scarlet and polished oak, with room and to spare in which to relax and talk with no fear of being overheard.

Wilkinson was waiting in the main lounge. His smile radiated welcome and it was the first welcome I'd seen for weeks. He took a step towards me from a table at which he'd been sitting. A low table with two deep armchairs and his own tipple half-consumed.

'What's your poison, Charles?' We shook hands. 'Nice of you to come.'

'Nice of you to ask me.' I matched him, grip for grip. 'I'll have whisky and water please, Bill.'

40

The hovering waiter took the order and we settled in the armchairs. It was first-name terms and without a hint of awkwardness. We sat in moderate luxury, relaxed and enjoyed ourselves.

He produced cheroots, offered the case to me then, when I declined, chose one for himself and lighted it.

'Cigarette?' he suggested. 'We can . . .'

'No. I usually smoke a pipe.'

'Go ahead, mate.' The ready grin touched his lips. 'Pipes. Solid dependability . . . I like the con.'

'Is it a con?' I fished pipe and tobacco from my pocket.

'The only real, one-hundred-per-cent bastard I ever knew. Never had a pipe from his teeth.'

'It's a con,' I agreed. 'I've known them, too.'

Such an easy man to get on with.

Think of armed bank robbers and the mind is with sub-humans, consumed by greed and willing to kill for mere cash. Not so. At least, not *always* so. Not this one. Not Wilkinson. Slightly rough-spoken, probably not too well-read, a moderate education, at best, but above all else *friendly*. Genuine. I think I never knew a more 'honest' – in the true sense of that word – man in my life.

He left his armchair long enough to move an ash-tray from a neighbouring table to our own. I noted that, too. The smooth, cat-like movement; crouched; arms, legs and body moving in a single, rhythmic flow. It was nothing – he was reaching for an ash-tray – but it wrote a book about the man's physical condition.

Then we sat and smoked, sipped booze and chatted as if we'd been friends for years.

Suddenly he said, 'Immediate reaction, Charles?'

'To what?'

'Me. You've been eyeing me enough.'

That, also, it seemed. He was *aware* . . . without being *obviously* aware.

I played my cards close to my chest.

'You can afford to smoke cheroots,' I smiled.

He chuckled. It was the sort of answer he liked and appreciated.

I added, 'You might even be able to afford the cheque.'

He nodded, this time very solemnly, then said, 'All right, let's talk about you. Married?'

'Married,' I admitted.

'What's the missus think?'

'She's not pleased.'

He raised questioning eyebrows.

'She's not yet convinced of my innocence,' I amplified.

I hesitated to go further than that. That she'd never *be* convinced was something I was coming to terms with, but a family matter and a subject not to be discussed with a stranger, however friendly that stranger might be.

'She doesn't know about you losing your job?'

'Not yet.' I paused, then added, 'The opportunity will arise.'

'I'm not married.'

'It has its advantages,' I murmured.

Again, he nodded understandingly and left it at that. The silence lasted all of five minutes, yet there was no mock-delicacy. It was a comfortable, almost cosy, silence. The silence of good companionship. The armchairs made for ease, the booze was like liquid silk, my pipe was drawing well and Wilkinson was obviously enjoying his cheroot.

It was one of those moments in life. You remember them. Not for anything dramatic or even out of the ordinary. You remember them for their quiet perfection; for their air of gentle conviviality. Those moments are important . . . if only because they're so rare.

Quite suddenly, he smiled and said, 'Masters – not you – should have been in the dock with us.'

'Masters!'

'The manager.'

'Good God!'

42

My surprise was quite genuine. I could have faulted Masters as a bank manager – in fact, I'd mentally faulted him scores of times in the past – but I hadn't doubted his honesty.

'Not deliberately,' continued Wilkinson quietly. 'He was never asked what was the best time to rob his bank. He just said . . . indirectly. At one of those social, all-men-together booze-ups he goes to. As innocent as you are, really. But *he* gave the info.'

'He should have known better.'

'Why?' Wilkinson moved a shoulder, then waved the hand holding the cheroot in a gentle, throw-away gesture. 'Human nature, mate. A bit of show-off. Who doesn't? No bloody harm.'

'You think not?'

'Not knowingly . . . that's what I mean.'

'That's a poor excuse.'

'What? Mention something to a trusted friend. Come on, Charles. We all do it.'

'Trusted . . . but not trustworthy,' I murmured.

'He didn't know. He was milked.'

'At least I'm pleased he wasn't deliberately dishonest.'

Wilkinson nodded silent understanding.

Damn the man! I was beginning to like him. Not merely accept him. *Like* him. Whatever he was, however big a scoundrel he was, he had his own brand of charm. Not the smooth, oily charm of a character out to wheedle his way into your good books. Nor the back-slapping charm (if it deserves the name) of the type with an ape-like approach. Wilkinson's charm had quiet, throw-away style. It was natural; a part of him and not an act put on for my benefit.

We sat in comfortable silence, sipping booze and smoking and, without making it obvious, I watched him and, basing my observations on the very many other men I'd faced and interviewed as a bank official, I tried to make some sort of assessment.

I imagined myself sitting behind my own desk in my old office. A tap on the door. The door opening and one of the junior clerks making the introduction.

'A Mr Wilkinson to see you, sir.'

'He has an appointment. Please ask him to step into the office.'

As he enters – as the clerk closes the door – I stand up and extend my hand. The normal, practised ploy. To note his manner of walk. (Assuming he has full use of both legs; no crutches, no necessary walking-sticks.) A firm walk? A timid walk? A hesitant walk? A busy, rushing walk? The walk that is little more than a stroll? An arrogant walk? A saunter? Three yards (thereabouts) to my outstretched hand. About three paces. Four, at most. But to a practised eye, the manner of covering those three yards can tell a lot.

At the same time, I take note of his dress.

His shoes? Black. Leather. Polished and well-cared-for. Not 'brothel creepers'. At a glance, moderately expensive shoes. His best, perhaps, and worn for my benefit. If so, that is not a bad thing; it shows good manners and a little thought . . . it also suggests an eventual request for a loan of some kind.

His clothes? A suit. Nothing casual; no take-it-or-leave-it attitude. Certainly not jeans! A suit of clerical grey; not a pattern giving the impression of a watered-down music-hall comedian's mode of dress. The trousers are neatly creased. The single-breasted jacket has its button fastened and there is no scattering of dandruff, or a stray strand of cotton where it shouldn't be. No breast-pocket handkerchief; not an important thing perhaps but (to me a personal foible) that hint of dressing-up-for-the-occasion . . . which smacks of *over*-dressing.

Clean-shaven. I have no axe to grind about facial hair, other than that I prefer it not to be there. Again, a personal thing. If a man's upper lip is heavy enough to carry a moustache, and the moustache is neatly trimmed, I am prepared to ignore my prejudice. Even beards, if properly shaped and trimmed. But merely to let hair *grow*. It can outweigh all other good impressions.

Finally, the hair. No modern 'with it' style, if you please. A straightforward, parted-on-one-side-then-brushed-back choice. A touch of cream to keep it in its place. Clean round the ears (no lamb-chop flamboyancy) and tapered at the nape.

A firm handshake, without it being a bone-crushing demonstration of strength.

'Please sit down, Mr Wilkinson.'

Now. Does he sit on the chair where it has been placed? (Which is a little too far from the desk for intimate conversation.) Or has he the presence of mind to move the chair a little nearer, but not *too* near?

This man – this William Wilkinson – impresses me. Before he has said a word, I like him and am prepared to listen to whatever he has to say with sympathy. Whatever his station in life, he has class. He has style. He is honest.

Then – almost casually – I open the file which is already on the desk in front of me. A quick glance at the top headings.

Occupation – BANK ROBBER.

My musings were interrupted.

A discreet waiter informed us that our lunch was ready.

'Thank you.' He rose from his chair, squashed what was left of the cheroot into a glass ash-tray, smiled and said, 'Charles.'

I tapped the last of the tobacco from my pipe into the ash-tray, then followed him out of the lounge, along the corridor and into the dining room.

The Ripon Spa Hotel dining room lives up to its three-star status. Tall windows look out upon well-kept parkland. The tables are spaced enough to ensure privacy. The linen is spotless, the cutlery, glassware and china are all sparklingly clean. The service can't be faulted and the food is Yorkshire-good ... which means it can't be bettered.

All this I knew – I'd eaten there before, therefore it didn't come as a surprise – but it was as delightful as ever.

The wine waiter came to the table and Wilkinson ordered.

'White wine with fish,' he smiled. 'Rhône Valley stuff. I think you'll like it, Charles.'

I made noises of approval. I knew little enough about wine, but already I knew enough about Wilkinson to leave the choice to him and the wine waiter. Thereafter the wine, the shrimp cocktail, the Dover sole and the gateau made a lunch fit for a monarch. Then the Viennese coffee, the cheddar and biscuits and the liqueur brandy. And Wilkinson ate and drank with the natural certainty of a man well-used to such fare.

We took the coffee, biscuits, cheese and liqueur in the lounge and, although we'd hardly said a word throughout the meal, I think the brandy loosened my tongue a little. Relaxed me more than usual, or at least gave me the courage – possibly the impudence – to ask questions I might otherwise have left unspoken.

'You seem to live well,' I observed.

'We've one life, mate. That's all.'

'Therefore, be comfortable?'

'Moderately.'

'Better than most – er – criminals.'

'I steal,' he said, simply.

'Of course.'

'From banks . . . and they can afford it.'

'It must be a wrench. Quite a contrast.' I smiled as I made the remark. 'This life-style, then prison life.'

'Prison?' he looked puzzled.

'At an educated guess, Dover sole isn't on the menu inside prison.'

'I've never been inside prison.' He returned the smile. 'I wouldn't know.'

'Forgive me.' I retained the smile and grew a little bolder. 'The police showed me a list of your previous convictions.'

'I don't lie, Charles.' I was his guest, therefore the criticism was mild . . . but unmistakable.

'The police showed me a list,' I insisted.

'*A* list.' He moved his shoulders. 'You trust the coppers too much, mate. They *do* lie . . . when it suits 'em. They'll show you a list of *anything*.'

'A false list?' I raised an eyebrow.

'If it suits 'em,' he repeated. 'If they want somebody nailed. A statement, maybe.'

'I made no statement,' I assured him.

'Course not. Why should you? You weren't in on it.' The moment of mild annoyance might never have been. He held out the case holding the cheroots. This time I accepted and dipped the end into the flame of the held-out lighter. Then, when we were both relaxed and smoking, he continued, 'Something of a shock to you, eh Charles?'

'Well . . .' I began awkwardly. 'It's not that . . .'

'No striped jersey. No sack with "Swag" printed on it.' He chuckled, amiably. Quietly.

'That's putting it strong,' I protested. 'But – all right – basically, that's what it boils down to.'

'It's what most people think.' He tasted the brandy and drew on the cheroot then, using the cheroot as baton-cum-pointer, he continued, 'Crime, Charles. You'd call me a criminal . . . right?'

'Yes,' I admitted quietly.

'So be it. Part-time criminal. We're pretty thick, underfoot. Semi-pro, you might say . . .'

'I'd say rather more than . . .'

'That's all, Charles. I'm *telling* you. Don't count the mugs. The mugs don't mean a bloody thing. Mugs fill prisons. They're not criminals. All they are is jerks who *want* to be criminals. They're mugs when they go in. Inside, they mix with mugs. When they come out, they're bigger mugs. You learn sod-all in prison.'

'I'll – er – take your word for it.'

'Straight.' He nodded his certainty. 'They think the Great Train Robbery was an off-the-cuff job. That's what mugs they are. It doesn't click with 'em. That crimes like that take years to set up. They won't have it. They're bloody barmy and they won't see what it takes to make a criminal craftsman.'

'They were caught,' I said tentatively.

'Who?'

'The train robbers.'

'*Some* were caught,' he said brusquely.

'Only "some"? I thought . . .'

'Forget it, Charles.'

'Eh?' I stared.

'You don't want to know about crime.'

'Ah, but I *do*.'

'No, just how the other half live. That's all.'

'Bill, I assure you . . .'

'Keep off it, mate.' The sudden, almost violent serious-ness caught me unawares. The ready smile was gone. It might never have been there. And yet there was a certain sad friendship in the way he looked at me. He seemed to be pleading, when he added, 'Keep clear of it, Charles. You've been well brought up . . . not like me.'

'That's crap. You could buy and sell me, and you know it.'

'What the hell has money to do with it?'

'Bill,' I said, solemnly, 'I have no friends. Just you . . . I think I count you as a friend. I'd like to. You're the only person I know who believes I'm not a crook.'

'You're not a crook,' he said, flatly.

'Okay . . . now, let's be friends.'

'Sure.'

But he didn't mean it. At least, he didn't *sound* to mean it. It was as if he'd suddenly remembered something. Suddenly realised he'd gone too far.

The impression was that it took a real effort to pull the scowl from his face before he raised a hand and brought a waiter to our table.

'Brandies . . . same again. And a fill-up of coffee.'

And that was it for that afternoon. The talk continued, but it meant nothing. Empty talk around hollow subjects. He'd closed and locked a door. He wasn't rude. Indeed, he was pleasant. But the easy flow of conversation had gone. And when we shook hands prior to parting I sensed reluctance on his part to re-visit The Spa in a week's time for another lunch . . . this time with me as host. But he agreed and, to that extent, I was happy.

I drove home as if returning from the office and for a few miles mentally re-lived a most unusual afternoon. I went over it hour at a time, word at a time.

Bill Wilkinson was a crook. A villain. Indeed by any yardstick he was a man I should, at least, despise . . . but, dammit, I *didn't*! Quite the reverse, in fact. I found myself wanting him as a friend. And that, too, was unusual. Until that moment I'd been proud of the fact that I was sufficient unto myself. Without being a deliberate loner, I'd never allowed anybody to get too close. I was Charles Ryder and, other than to my family, that's all I was. Politeness demanded that I be civil to neighbours and acquaintances, but beyond that I'd never been prepared to go. Never *wanted* to go.

But now . . .

There was no logic in it. Certainly the £5,000 had no bearing on my feelings. Just the man – just Wilkinson – his lack of guile and his cheerful acceptance of what he was. Nor was it the novelty of knowing and breaking bread with a self-confessed criminal. I'd known criminals before; men whose criminality had been more subtle – whose wheeling and dealing had, perhaps, been a mere hair's-breadth on the right side of the law – but whose amorality had been greater than that of Bill Wilkinson. I'd known them and scorned them. I'd sat in silent judgement on them, and found them wanting.

Why, then, this man? Why Bill Wilkinson?

The answer wasn't there or, if it was, I couldn't find it. Only that I wanted to meet him again. And again and again. That I wanted our friendship to blossom and grow . . . and, for the life of me, I couldn't find a reason worthy of the name.

And, from the subject of friendship, my thoughts moved to the subject of marriage. My marriage.

I wondered how long I could continue this folly. This stupid deceit of 'going to the office' each day. There had to be an end to it, and in the not-too-distant future, if only for financial reasons. I wasn't a rich man, and I was living on what savings I'd been able to accumulate over the years, plus the severance pay. I had a monthly mortgage to meet, Anne (albeit unwittingly) was continuing her accustomed standard of living and both Judy and Tim took it for granted that the cash for school expenses and pleasures was available as before.

Weeks? Oh yes, I could count it in weeks – but not months – then the truth would have to be told. And *then* . . .

I honestly didn't know. The truth was, I daren't give it much thought. I suppose I viewed the money Bill Wilkinson had given me as a sort of safety-net. Ready cash, with which to meet the expense of . . .

A divorce?

I almost refused the word room in my thoughts, but it was there. It was far more than a possibility. More than a probability. Anne was convinced she was the wife of a thief, and what love we'd once had for each other had gradually

50

turned to mere acceptance. And *that* wouldn't keep us together. That wouldn't carry the strain. A bleak outlook, and every day made things worse.

For a man supposedly versed in money-matters, I was behaving like an idiot. When I thought of it – when I forced myself to think of it – I was terrified. Almost panic-stricken.

Therefore, tonight. This evening. When I arrived home, I was going to have it out with Anne. Whatever the emotional cost, however many tears and accusations. She'd be told. Then Tim and Judy. The truth – everything – and whether they believed or disbelieved didn't matter too much. Dammit, the marriage was in tatters and beyond repair. So . . . what matter?

I was shattered to find how *much* it mattered!

I found myself trembling, as if weak from a long illness. The decision had been made, and the realisation seemed to drive strength from my body. *The* decision. But what of all the other decisions which of necessity now had to be faced? What about Judy? What about Tim? What about so many other things a divorce would spew up?

Circles within circles. An echo without an end.

I was a danger to other drivers. My road-concentration was about zero. The lay-by was coming up. I flicked the trafficator and glanced in the rear-view mirror. I saw the car – the white car with the blue, inverted-flower-pot-shaped light on its roof – but I gave it no thought. It didn't even register . . . not really. My mind was filled with other things. More important – more personal – things.

I stopped the car, turned off the ignition and eased the tightness of the safety harness. I gripped the top of the wheel, lowered my forehead onto my clenched fists and tried to find sense in what seemed to be everlasting lunacy.

A marriage was a marriage . . . no more. A legal mating. It was *never* more than that. A contract of fidelity, wrapped up in religious mumbo-jumbo. Damnation, *that's all it was*. That at the most. The Humphrey Bogart/Ingrid Bergman/

51

Casablanca thing was a fairy tale, fit only for emotional kindergarteners. It didn't happen that way. It *never* happened that way. Never *had*. It couldn't . . .

In that case, why the hell were the sobs tearing their way through my body and making my shoulders heave? Why were the tears pushing their way past closed lids and running down my cheeks?

I both heard and felt the door alongside me open, but again it didn't register. Even when I was hauled from the car. For the moment it meant nothing.

'Is it him?'

'Yes, it's him. It's Ryder.'

'Stand up, Ryder. Come on, stand up. Don't mess us about.'

'Watch his hands.'

'Don't worry.'

'What the hell's wrong with him? Is he drunk?'

'God knows. Come on, Ryder. Don't . . .'

Perhaps I went a little mad. A little berserk. Perhaps I *was* a little mad. I wouldn't argue the point. I regained what I suppose must be called 'realisation' with a rush, saw uniforms I hated worn by two men who were apparently trying to assault me. I fought back. Lashed out. Kicked and fisted, until handcuffs held my hands behind my back.

One of them gasped, 'You bastard,' then kneed me in the balls . . . and that was the end of *my* puny resistance.

'Quite the little Yorkshire Ripper.' The detective chief inspector smiled, but there was no geniality in the smile. Self-satisfaction, yes. But no mirth. 'Quite the poor man's Al Capone.'

His name was Smith. Maybe they spelled it with an 'i', maybe they spelled it with a 'y'. I wouldn't know. I never bothered to find out. As far as I was concerned, they spelled it with a 'b'. B-a-s-t-a-r-d.

The man was openly enjoying himself. He was talking in

riddles, but that didn't matter. *He* understood . . . and nobody else mattered.

Me? I was only the miserable piece of dog-dirt he was talking to. He'd missed me on the bank raid, but that was okay. This time he had me by the short hairs. This time, he *had* me, and he was enjoying watching me squirm.

'Where's the gun?' he purred.

'I don't know what the hell . . .'

'Cut it!' Imagine a whispered scream. That was it. I was allowed to say what *he* wanted me to say. That or nothing. 'Don't come the crap with me, Ryder. Not this time. I need that gun. The hard way, the easy way.' The smile came and went. 'Unofficially, I'd prefer the hard way.'

'I haven't a gun,' I muttered.

'Not *with* you, but where?'

'It's at the club. Where it always is. Locked away.'

'Not *that* gun.'

The man was crazy. Crazy with hatred . . . maybe like all coppers. I squinted at him, with some difficulty through my half-closed eyes. I wondered what the devil my face looked like. The nose had gone. A smack across the bridge with a police truncheon doesn't leave much doubt, and the swelling which was closing my eyes merely underlined what I already guessed. But, strangely, not much pain. A numbness and a half-refusal to quite believe what had happened, or even what was happening, and complete ignorance of its cause.

'Am I under arrest?' I croaked.

'Oh, no.' The sarcasm wasn't even subtle. 'We've brought you in to congratulate you, lad. To give you a bloody medal.'

'Two police patrolmen jumped me . . .'

'We can handle that later, Ryder. Assault on Police. Resisting Arrest. Those are just cherries on top of the Knickerbocker Glory.'

The room. That infernal room. I recognised it from the

past. From Smith's previous hounding and interrogation. The name on the door read Interview Room, but it was *Smith's* room. The room in which he committed the foulness he called policing. Detecting crime . . . the 'Smith' way. Believing nothing. Never being wrong. A chamber of artful horrors, presided over by this damned detective chief inspector.

'What have I *done*?' I breathed.

'Nothing . . . that's why you're here.'

'What am I *supposed* to have done?'

'Careful, Ryder,' he warned gently. 'Tread very carefully. We're alone, remember that. That face of yours – those ribs of yours, that hand of yours – and other bits and pieces – one more broken bone wouldn't be noticed.'

'Coppers did that. I still don't know why the hell . . .'

'Don't treat me like a complete pillock, Ryder. Not again. I won't stand it twice.'

'Please!' I pleaded. 'Why? In God's name *why*?'

'Your daughter says you've been at the bank all day.'

'Oh!'

'Your *son* says you've been at the bank all day.'

'Why should you . . .'

'But *we* know you haven't . . . don't we, Ryder?'

'Look, why should you . . .'

'*We* know you haven't worked a single day at the bank since you and your pals lifted that lovely two-hundred-thousand quid . . . don't we, Ryder?'

The chickens were all coming home to roost. Every last one of them. But they weren't chickens any more. They were pterodactyles, with their jaws wide open and their claws eager for flesh.

'*We* know where you've been this afternoon, don't we Ryder? *We* know who shot your bloody wife.'

'Shot my . . .' I gaped. I couldn't believe. This mad copper was making things up. Framing me for something. Fixing me as nobody had ever been fixed before. I moaned,

'Smith, you can't do this. Even *you* can't. . .'

'*I can*! I bloody-well *will*.' He lowered his face until it was less than twelve inches from my own. I could smell his blasted breath – despite my own broken nose – as he crooned, 'Ryder, you're under. You've gone down for the third time. We have statements from your kids. You hated each other. You couldn't lie to her. She wouldn't believe you . . . that's why you hated her. That's why you hated each other. That's why you went back, this afternoon, and shot her.'

'No!' You've got it wrong. You're . . .'

'Where's the gun, Ryder? *Where's the flaming gun*?'

What the hell had I to lose? This wasn't a bluff on the part of Smith. It was far too big an accusation for bluff. This sweet bastard was busy hanging a murder charge around my neck . . . *and* he'd bust a gut to make it stick. So, what was one more copper more or less?

I straightened up from the chair and, as I did so, I peered through half-closed eyes and aimed the dome of my skull dead-centre for his face. I hit the bull (in more ways than one) and he bowled over and sprawled on the floor of the room. The object was to prevent him from yelling for reinforcements, and I swung a shoe at the side of his head. For a second it felt as if a chain-saw had touched my side, and I knew what he'd meant by the remark about 'those ribs of yours'. No matter. I followed through and he was out cold before he could open his mouth.

I leaned against the table, caught my breath and tried to come to terms with the gathering pain. For sure I was tempted. I *could* have finished him off, there and then. I had a chair, I had my hands, I had enough homicidal rage. I *could* have finished him off, but the delay might have cost me what slender chance of freedom I'd given myself.

I knew that police station. I knew that Interview Room. God, I knew it as well as I knew my own home. There was a corridor beyond the door, and the corridor led to a back entrance from the car park. The car park – it was an official police car park, which wasn't too well lit and dusk had thickened into near-night, and that car park was about the most deserted area of tarmac in all Haggthorpe. Get into the corridor without being seen. Out through the door and into the car park. Take things a step at a time.

From the car park, into the shadows along the side of the police station. From there? Bill Wilkinson had mentioned the Great Train Robbery. *They'd* used a farm not too far from the scene of the crime. The object had been to sit it out and let the search flow past them. It hadn't worked . . . but the idea had merit.

Almost directly opposite the police station were public toilets. They were *there* – not much more than thirty yards from where I was standing – and if I could reach *them* . . .

I reached them.

I locked myself in one of the bogs, stayed there the rest of the night, all next day and into the small hours of the following morning.

It was not funny. Indeed, it was one of the most *un*funny few hours of my life.

Few hours!

It was an eternity.

I crept from the toilets, more dead than alive.

For thirty hours (thereabouts) I'd sat with my back against one wall and my feet against the other. Knees bent. Cold, miserable and in pain. For some of the time I'd been, not asleep, but in a state of semi-consciousness. Five or six times I'd roused myself sufficiently enough to flush the toilet and splash ice-cold water onto my face. The pain in my side was bad. I didn't doubt I had a cracked rib – perhaps more than one – but I dredged what comfort I could from the knowledge that these days the medics no longer strap such injuries; the modern treatment is rest, warmth and as little movement as possible . . . and at least I didn't move much. My hand? The left hand was badly bruised and swollen. I could move my fingers a little, therefore I didn't think bones were broken. I worked to remember where the injury had been caused, but couldn't. A slammed squad car door, perhaps? That, at a guess.

The rest? I didn't know. I'd had neither room nor energy to explore. I knew I ached all over, that my face throbbed and that my side felt as if a blunt knife was being driven home . . . but most of all I felt fury.

As I forced my agonised body from shadow to shadow – as I painfully sought the outskirts of the town – the main emotion was blinding rage. It did much to counter the pain. It forced me forward, and demanded that I rest and recover before demanding some form of retribution.

Odd. I had to deliberately *remember* that Anne had been murdered. It should have filled my thoughts, but didn't. Pain filled my thoughts, and what room there was left was taken up by the self-promise of vengeance.

Dawn was lightening the east when I found a place to rest. The 'For Sale' sign reminded me. It was a large house, on the very fringe of the town, standing in its own grounds. It had been unoccupied for months. Stables and outbuildings were at the rear, and for once fortune smiled on me. One of the outbuildings was unlocked. I found the haft of a broken spade and used it to hold the door closed.

Then I slept.

This time it was real sleep. Dream-haunted, but restful. I found straw and sacking, and that was enough. From behind the pain, I argued that this place must have already been searched. It was a calculated risk, and I took it. For the moment, daylight was my enemy, and in addition I was weak and in no condition to pick and choose. I slept in filth . . . but I slept.

My watch showed 6 p.m. when I hauled myself to my

feet. Light still filtered through the dusty, webbed window, but nobody had disturbed me.

The rest had refreshed me. I was both hungry and thirsty, but my face and head had eased to a steady ache, and my side and hand were stiff, but unless I moved too rapidly were bearable. I was able to stitch ideas together and plan.

The countryside. Well clear of Haggthorpe. The Dales, perhaps? Yes . . . I decided on the Dales. Not Nidderdale or Wharfedale or any of the better known dales though. It was late May and the tourists were arriving in increasing numbers. I wanted one of the smaller, less commercialised dales. One few people knew about, but at the same time somewhere within easy distance of villages. Somewhere I knew. I weighed the pro's and the con's and decided upon Skelldale. One of the lesser-known offshoots from Nidderdale. It led nowhere. You went to Skelldale to *visit* Skelldale; to call at a dale hamlet then return. I knew it. We'd spent sunny, summer days there. Anne and the kids and myself. Not recently, but in the past. In the happier past, before the world – *my* world – had turned rotten on me.

Before I'd been daubed a bank robber. Before Anne had been murdered.

God! I'd almost *forgotten*.

I remembered, but the memory brought little mental anguish.

In retrospect, I think *that* was when I first realised the change in myself. I was able to think of Anne – even to accept that I *had* loved her – and to know she'd been shot to death without real sorrow. My own touch of hell had brutalised me. Basically, I didn't give a damn about anybody other than myself . . . and this time it was no put-on.

She was dead. Okay, she was dead, but we all die and in time somebody would pay. Meanwhile I was alive. Alive and, gradually, becoming more alive. Free, and would remain free. I'd make it. By God, I'd make it! I'd live and people – certain people – would regret that I *had* lived.

I waited until eleven o'clock; until the drinkers had made their way homewards and the traffic on the roads had eased. By that time the rain was bucketing down. It came in clouds of water and, as I stood in shelter and shadow, I could see the waves of rain sweeping past the orange of the sodium street-lighting. No matter . . . I'd already survived more than a soaking.

I took one of the sacks, and used it as a combined head-piece and shoulder-covering. What I looked like didn't matter. If possible, I was going to move unseen. Like a fox or a stoat – like a wild thing – I'd be *there*, but nobody would see me.

I ducked from gate to gate until I reached the end of the sodium lamps. From then on, blackness other than the illumination from car headlamps. I played tag with them, and always won because I could see their reflection before they arrived. Up the rise, beyond the town, then over a rail-and-post fence and into the fields. The spring grass was ankle-length and sodden and, for what good they were, I might as well have not been wearing shoes. I kept parallel to the road; knees and shoulders bent; pumping forward, field-length at a time. I sought gates, then swung back towards the road. When I couldn't find gates I searched for weaknesses in hedges and bulldozed my way through. A few thorn-scratches didn't matter. Each step took me a few more inches towards freedom, and freedom was worth any price. Any discomfort. Any pain.

The hunger left me. The thirst left me. (Who the hell could be thirsty in that downpour?) One foot forward, then the other foot forward. That's all that mattered. That was all I lived for, and my sole reason for having been born.

I tried to focus in on my watch as I swam back into consciousness. I didn't recognise the hand at the end of the

59

wrist. Could any hand be so filthy? So caked in mud and blood? So swollen and disfigured? Not my hand. Christ . . . not *my* hand.

But it was. And the torn, scarecrow-sleeve of the jacket was from *my* jacket, too. It shouldn't have been. It had never been before, but it was now.

I back-tracked my memory and vaguely remembered my knees buckling. The pitching forward. The sprawling onto the soaked grass . . . then the blackness.

The watch showed a few minutes after six and, beyond the watch, the pale blue of early-morning sky was naked of even a wisp of cloud. But it was cold and *I* was cold – bone-deep cold – and the grass and my clothes were still saturated. The sky was pulling a con trick. It *had* rained. It had belted down most of the night . . . and now it was past dawn and I was out in the open for anybody and everybody to see.

I'd worked during those darkness hours. Christ, how I'd worked! Pushing forward, hammering ahead, seeking some unknown sanctuary before morning. Where was it? Skelldale? How the hell could *I* ever make Skelldale? What sort of blind lunacy made me think . . .

'And holy Jesus what have we got here?'

The Irish twang gave the words a laughing lilt. Robbed them of real surprise and denied them the ability to frighten. But I didn't need that, and the words didn't need that. I hadn't control enough of my senses to be surprised. Only curious.

I turned my head, saw the tilted barrels of a twelve-bore and beyond them the face. Dark-skinned beneath the unshaven cheeks and jaw. Dark-eyed and black-haired. Lips bent and teeth peeping in a carefree grin.

'And by God that must have been one hell of a fight.' Then the chuckle, and the repeated, 'One *hell* of a fight.'

I wanted to say something. I didn't know what. Just anything. A plea for sympathy, perhaps. Help? I don't think help. I didn't expect *help* from anybody. Nobody –

nobody in the world – was going to help *me*. But I wanted to say *something* . . . but lacked the strength.

I didn't have to.

As he bent, he murmured, 'Come on, bucko. I can't leave you here now, can I? My old mother would never forgive me.'

He didn't actually carry me to the caravan in that I was upright alongside him. But as near as dammit and without much effort.

'My old mother.' Or, as he said it, 'Me auld moother.' To me that phrase will always equate with compassion. Unquestioning and unqualified compassion.

His name was Kelly – Tommy Kelly – and he was, I suppose, an Irish tinker. A 'travelling man'. What the north countryman would call a 'dyddacoy'. There might have been a touch of Romany blood in him, but if so only enough to darken the skin and blacken the hair; the Kelly family were too down-to-earth for cards, tea-leaves or crystal balls. Kelly, his wife Seonad and his four children left their mark, wherever they paused. They created small havoc in their passing. The fire, between the van and the tent, was never low and it was fuelled by wood torn from gates and fencing.

Yet their wisdom almost amounted to magic. They could name a bird from its wing-flap. Forecast the weather by sniffing the breeze. Pinpoint a roosting pheasant by hearing its call.

For almost a fortnight, Seonad nursed me back to health. Herb poultices drove out the pain. Thick broth and what at first I took to be chicken, but which turned out to be rabbit, returned my strength. And never a question and never a hesitation.

We had common ground. Like me, they hated the police. Tommy called them 'the powliss' and when he mouthed the word it was like a spat curse.

One day we sat facing each other on the shafts of the van.

61

Tommy smoked herb tobacco in his battered pipe and, for perhaps fifteen minutes, we were content with the silence of each other's company.

Then, very softly, he said, 'Charlie, my boy, if the police came what would you do?'

'Run,' I replied shortly.

'And would you tell me why?'

'No.'

'And why's that? Because you don't want me to know?'

'Because I don't want you to be involved.'

'Friendship? Is that it?'

'Friendship,' I agreed.

'Now, there's a fine thing.' He eyed the split stem of his pipe. 'My old mother would have scratched your eyes out. Putting such a small price on friendship.'

The silence lasted for a few minutes, then I murmured, 'Killing.'

'Killing, is it?'

'I didn't . . . but the police think I did.'

'The police?' He sniffed. 'That's like the Holy Bible saying you *didn't*.'

'I didn't,' I repeated.

'Was it just before we met?' he probed.

'Before you found me?'

'Before we met,' he insisted.

'No.' I smiled. 'I'd escaped from police custody.'

'By God! And how many of the buggers did you cripple?'

'They crippled me.'

'They would, too.' He nodded soberly. 'The devils. They'd enjoy doing it.'

Late that afternoon he struck and packed the tent, loaded the van and harnessed the horse between the shafts. By dusk we'd left even the B-class roads and were out in the wilds, God knows where. Too far from the Haggthorpe police for them to bother us. At a guess, somewhere rarely visited, perhaps not even *known*, by any police officer.

The family never questioned Tommy's decisions. The

only schooling the children needed was that which would enable them to live lives like their parents, and Seonad was no feminist. She'd chosen her man, and he was a good man and she was wise enough to leave it at that.

At night I slept in the tent with the children. It was a good tent; quite weather-proof; army-surplus, at a guess, with a thick groundsheet. We slept in bedrolls, and Seonad had the knack of making them as comfortable as feathers.

I'd never camped out in my life before, but this wasn't camping out. This was *living* out. It had different rhythms. Different sleep patterns. Slumber came in short spells, but it was deep and refreshing. Beyond the partly-open flap the fire spat and flamed. Beyond the fire was the caravan, with the top half of the door always open. I'd lie and watch. Warm and comfortable. Half-asleep. I'd see Tommy come from the caravan to fuel the fire; hear the soft chink of the tether-chain as the horse sought new grass; smell the tang of burning wood mixed with air as heady as champagne.

At dawn − sometimes just before dawn − I'd watch Tommy come from the van. Fully dressed and carrying his twelve-bore. Then I'd wait for the distant thump − sometimes the double-thump − and know we'd have meat for lunch.

Make no mistake. Tommy and his kind live well. I know. I shared that life. Rabbit, hare, duck, pheasant, partridge. Sometimes chicken . . . if somebody had been foolish enough to leave the hen-house unlocked. Once, hedgehog; it tasted a little like chicken, but with a gamey flavour. And of course eggs and vegetables. Hen eggs, duck eggs, goose eggs, and eggs from some of the larger game birds. Vegetables straight from the store or the soil. All spiced with wild herbs.

And every day I hurt a little less and grew a little stronger.

On Tuesday, June 9th . . .

I'd lost all recollection of either day or date, but it was a beautiful morning, and I felt fitter than I'd ever felt in my life. I'd worked it out. It was a six-to-one shot against it being Sunday, and I wanted to get in touch with the world again.

I strolled to where Tommy was squatting, gutting and cleaning a mallard, and tried to find words that wouldn't hurt. It was impossible. It had to be said and saying it would wound . . . but it had to *be* said.

'Is there a village near here?' I asked gently.

'Five miles.'

He didn't look up. I think he guessed what was coming, but he concentrated his attention on the razor-sharp knife as it spilled the guts from the duck.

'Is there a shop there?'

He nodded, and continued his task.

'What sort of a shop?'

'Post Office.'

'Do they sell newspapers?'

'Charlie boy.' He flipped the knife and it stood, half-blade deep, in the earth. He tilted his head. 'What would you be wanting with a newspaper?'

'World War Three could have started. We wouldn't know.'

'And if we *did* know?'

'You know what I mean, Tommy.'

'No.' He dropped the mallard and straightened as he spoke. 'I can't read writing, Charlie. Just pictures. And, I tell you, I've never seen a picture worth looking at twice. The buggers out there . . .' He jerked his head. 'I wouldn't give them the sweat from my brow.'

'It's where I belong, Tommy.'

'The devil it is. You belong here, bucko. They arsed you out, remember?'

'They arsed me out,' I agreed. 'They broke me, and you've mended me. And I'm grateful. Eternally grateful.'

'Like my old mother used to say. Gratitude buys

64

bugger-all.'

'Your old mother was a wise old lady.'

'That she was.'

'What would she say now?'

'I'm damned if I know.' He compressed his lips, then muttered, 'I'm damned if I can ask her . . . God rest her soul.'

I turned and walked away. He knew. No more needed to be said. That's how close we'd become; how fine-tuned we were to each other's thoughts and feelings. That, too, was part of Tommy Kelly's world.

He disappeared after the midday meal. I knew where he'd gone. I think Seonad knew, too, but nobody said anything. There was just this air of unaccustomed misery about the camp. Like waiting at the death-bed of a close friend.

He returned late that afternoon and tossed a copy of *The Yorkshire Post* onto my lap.

'You'll let me know,' he said, with a wry grin.

'What's that?'

'Whether it has. Then we'll all know.'

'What?'

'World War Three. Whether the buggers have started blowing each others heads off.'

'I'll let you know,' I smiled.

I opened the newspaper and noticed the date. Tuesday, June 9th . . .

I saw Tommy leave the van with his gun at a few minutes after dawn. I closed my eyes to catch another hour of sleep, and was awakened by Seonad calling my name. I climbed upright, dressed and ducked out of the tent.

'You should go, Charlie,' she said sadly. She held out a mug of steaming coffee as she spoke. 'If you're going, you should go before Tommy gets back. He'd like it that way.'

'No tearful leave-takings?' I curled my fingers around the

warm mug and tasted the coffee.

'If you *have* to go.'

I gulped more coffee, then said, 'The clothes. The boots, trousers, jacket. They're Tommy's. I'll . . .'

'He doesn't give and want back.'

'No. I'm sorry.'

'You could stay,' she said gently. 'The kids like you. Tommy likes you.' She paused, then added, 'I like you.'

'I'm bad news,' I mumbled. 'The police want me for murder, and a bastard called Smith will make sure it sticks.'

We stood in awkward silence for a few minutes. I was tempted. Who wouldn't have been? I'd received casual, almost throw-away kindness from this family. The brand of kindness you take without embarrassment. The brand you can't buy. Can't really *earn*. I think they'd saved my life. They'd certainly ensured my freedom. And now . . .

I cleared my throat and said, 'As Tommy's old mother might have said . . .'

'She wouldn't.' She was gazing at the brightening sky on the horizon. 'An orphanage in County Fermanagh. That's as far back as his memory goes. He never knew his mother. Never knew his mother *or* his father . . .'

'Oh!'

'. . . And now that's something else you know, nobody else knows.'

'Seonad, I wish you hadn't . . .'

'Why not?' She turned and faced me. There wasn't hatred there. Only sadness. But so *much* sadness. She reached behind her, took a string-tied purse from the van steps and tossed it towards me. As I caught it, she said, 'Tommy says take it, so take it. We don't use paper-money. If the van catches fire paper gets burned. I'm sorry if it's heavy, but . . .'

'Good God, I can't . . .'

'Take it, Charlie. It isn't *worth* anything.'

I think – I *hope* – the quick smile carried forgiveness. Then she mounted the steps and closed both flaps of the van behind her.

I was in Pendlebridge by just after four. I'd walked, cadged a lift in a farm Land Rover and caught a couple of local buses. On my way I'd bought soap and towel, toothbrush and toothpaste and a small, zip-up bag. I'd also booked in for bed and breakfast at one of the less flash Pendlebridge guest houses.

Pendlebridge. It conned itself into believing it was an inland holiday spot. It was nothing of the sort. It was a one main street market town and the railway station or bus stop for rock-climbers and fell-walkers. My own untidy beard and long hair were not alone. Even the hard-wear crumple of my clothes was matched. This was the gateway to the Great Outdoors and hirsute scarecrows shambled around and rubbed shoulders with the locals without causing comment. An 'olde-worlde-country-crafte' place, and the only spot I knew where I'd have been accepted without stares. A place where limited metamorphosis could be arranged without attracting attention.

I found a hairdresser's shop. Strictly speaking, a 'barber's'. No blow-waves here; only variants on the old fashioned short-back-and-sides. That was okay. It went with the clothes. It went with the partly-grown beard.

I examined myself in the mirror as the scissors snipped. Was I different? Had I altered? I thought so. Enough. The broken nose, the whiskers, the hair, the tanned skin. The face, too, or so I thought. The swelling had broadened the cheeks a little. It hadn't all gone away, nor ever would. There was enough to make those who'd known me pass me in the street without recognising me. At least, I thought so. I *hoped* so.

I had a snack-meal in a café complete with juke-box and teenage layabouts. Beans on toast. What else? Seonad would have committed hara-kiri.

Then I found a kiosk, checked with Directory Enquiries and telephoned Bill Wilkinson.

'Charles! Where the hell . . .'

'Don't ask too many questions, Bill. Just listen.'

Among other things, my cheque book was at Haggthorpe Police Station, but I'd worked things out. Bill had a good solicitor; good enough, I hoped, to march into the lion's den and demand my property. Then Bill could send the cheque book to me, I'd make a cheque out to him, he'd bank it, draw ready money out of his own account and forward *that* onto me. It needed time, and it needed trust . . . but I had all the rest of my life.

I gabbled it all off to Bill, gave the address of the guest house, then ended, 'That's it, Bill. Can you do it?'

'Sure, but . . .'

'You have the address?'

'Sure, but . . .'

'Don't tell anybody. Nobody. Understand that?'

'Okay, okay, but . . .'

'And don't try to get in touch. Smith might be watching.'

'Okay, Charles, but . . .'

I dropped the receiver and cut him short.

Okay, I was getting a little paranoic about Smith. But he was out to nail me, and the last time we'd been close I'd butted him in the face. I didn't want to wake up one morning and find him looking down at me.

I'd tried to angle it from Smith's viewpoint. As far as *he* was concerned, Bill and I were buddies; we'd been buddies long enough for me to work with him in the bank hold-up. Wherever he was, Smith yearned like hell to get his hands on my collar. Telephone tapping? I wasn't up on the do's and don'ts, but it seemed a possibility and, if so, there was an address to play with.

It was wasting money – Tommy's money – but I had to be both sure and safe. I hurried to the guest house, told some yarn about having been in touch with home and learning of a sudden illness, paid for the bed and breakfast I wasn't going to have, mentioned that a parcel might arrive for me within the next few days, collected my few belongings, then headed for the open countryside.

Smith, you see, The next time I saw Smith, it had to be on *my* terms. And alone. And after he'd been made to sweat, *and* after he'd nailed the bastard who'd murdered Anne.

For ten days – ten not-too-comfortable nights – I slept in Dutch barns. The farmers around Pendlebridge seemed to favour them, and most of them had bales upon which to rest. It was little more than cat-napping and Tommy's tent was five-star luxury by comparison, but the rhythm had been established and I was up and away before dawn. On the Friday I found a Picnic Area, not too far from the town, with cold-water, wash-bowl facilities in the toilets and I could spruce myself up a little before venturing into the crowds.

I spent most of the days at the bus terminal. In the waiting room. I could see the guest house at an angle through one of the windows. I watched for postmen, but more importantly I watched for policemen.

I bought myself soap, a towel, a comb and a clothes-brush. I allowed myself one main meal a day; the obligatory fry-up at one of the chips-with-everything, cheapjack cafés. It was a lousy life and, more than once, I was tempted to up sticks and make my way back to where I'd left the Kelly family, but knowing Tommy and his peculiar pride, I argued that he'd already have moved on and, if *he* didn't want me to find him, I'd search in vain.

On the Monday I telephoned the guest house.

Yes, there was a letter for me. A letter, not a parcel. Yes, they'd keep it until I collected it.

I passed the end of the road three times. Passed the guest house twice, on the opposite pavement. I was like a cat on broken glass. It was dark when I collected the manilla envelope. There was no letter. Just the cheque book.

The next morning I posted a cheque for £1,000 to Bill. £1,000 from the £5,000 he'd given me. I had a word with the post office people; told them I was walking the fells and arranged for them to be poste restante for my mail. I enclosed a short note with the cheque, telling Bill to forward the cash to the post office.

Then it was back to Dutch barns, and as low a profile as possible.

On Saturday, June 20th, the cash arrived. First (indeed the only) delivery. One hundred tenners, all used notes, packed tight in a cigar box.

That was the last night I spent in a Dutch barn.

It was like shaking off shackles. I had money. I was free. I could move around.

That Sunday (the 21st) I moved out of the Dales. Out of Yorkshire. I caught a train from Pendlebridge to Leeds, then a train from Leeds to Preston.

God knows where, or when, I made the re-appraisal. Gradually, I think. It might have started when I was with Tommy and Seonad; by example, they'd shown me what freedom really meant. It was their sort of freedom and, although at the time it had been idyllic, some buried grain of logic inside me had warned me that it was not my sort of freedom. Being wise after the event, I tend to think the slow change of direction started then. I'm prepared to believe that the nights in Dutch barns accelerated it. Whatever I'd thought on my first dash for freedom, I was *not* a 'beast of the field'. I was very much a town animal, always had been and always would be. With the Kelly family, Tommy had been the hunter and the forager, Seonad had taken what he brought home and had provided food. Me? I'd been a guest. Alone – as had been proved since my arrival at Pendlebridge – I needed cafés and at night I'd been without comfort.

I can only guess at when the change of heart took place, or even started, but for sure, when I saw those ten-pound notes stacked away in the cigar box, the final decision to reach for what I called 'civilisation' was not a hard one.

I deliberately timed it to reach Preston in the small hours of Monday morning. I napped on the train and at Preston sought warmth and a minimum of comfort in the station waiting room. At 8.30 a.m. I enjoyed bacon and eggs at a tiny café, then toured the shops, buying things.

By mid-afternoon I was presentable. Cleaned up, decently shod, decently clothed and with a suitcase holding spare clothes and toiletries. I felt a new man. I most certainly *was* a re-emerged man. This time I chose a modest restaurant, and as I enjoyed a nicely cooked, nicely served meal, I pondered my way through the various possibilities.

London was out. I had the Northerner's inbuilt fear of the Smoke. It was *too* big. Had I known it well, I might have thought differently, but like most of my kind, the only London *I* knew – the only London in which I wasn't completely lost – was bounded by the City limits and the West End. My London was the tourist's London . . . and not even all of that.

I wanted somewhere with people. Villages, hamlets, even market towns were all too dangerous. Other than at places like Pendlebridge, strangers tended to be gawped at, and Pendlebridge was too near Smith for relaxed comfort.

A population then and, if possible, a shifting population. Blackpool?

Blackpool fitted the bill, but . . .

I couldn't put my finger on that 'but', other than that I had an instinctive feeling that Blackpool *wasn't* the place. Maybe the population was *too* shifting. The obvious place in which a criminal on the run might seek sanctuary. Which, logically, meant the police would be everlastingly vigilant. What *I* could figure out, *they* could figure out. I

71

wanted quieter, more contented cops. I also wanted somewhere with a permanent population whose number didn't include as many hoteliers, guest house proprietors and the like. Blackpool was a holiday resort. Some people thought *the* holiday resort. Other than catering for holiday-makers its industry was virtually nil, and few people retired there.

Those were some of the reasons, but they didn't add up to the total. There was something else, but I couldn't name it.

But thinking of Blackpool – thinking of people *not* retiring there – brought the answer.

Southport. Like Blackpool, a holiday resort with a shifting population, but not *only* a holiday resort. People retired there. People lived there; people who worked in Liverpool or even Manchester. It was a seaside town, but also a commuting town.

Having decided, I paid for the meal and returned to the railway station.

Southport accepted me. It almost embraced me. A middle-class town, with upper-middle-class manners, it reminded me of Haggthorpe. It flaunted its so-called 'millionaire's row' and kept its seedy, Victorian red-brick tucked away up side-streets. It boasted one of the finest row of shops in the UK, but take a turning away from the sea and the gimcrack dumps were waiting to rob you blind. It had a stretch of sands any resort would have been proud of, but with Fleetwood to the north and the Mersey to the south, they were never quite *clean*.

That was Southport . . . and still is Southport.

I knew banking, I had a valid cheque book and I knew my account number at Haggthorpe Nat West. Within a month, every penny I owned had been transferred to the Southport branch of my new bank, I had a new cheque book and I had a banker's card. By today's yardstick, I existed.

Tim and Judy?

I fear I gave them little thought. They belonged to another world. When I'd needed their support, they'd both let me down. Badly. They'd accepted everything and offered nothing, and now it was *my* turn to offer nothing. Nor did my conscience prick me. The re-birth was complete . . . and they wouldn't starve.

That first night, I found a self-contained flat. Meant as a holiday flat, it was at least half a mile from the promenade, and therefore not the first choice of holiday-makers. It was part of a rambling house, owned and caretakered by an elderly biddy who jumped at the idea of a permanent resident; in fact, I rented it on a month-to-month basis, always with the option on the following month. It had a fair-sized bedroom, complete with double-bed and furniture and a shower-room-cum-wash-room en suite, a decent lounge and an adequate kitchenette. There was a hall, of sorts, with a toilet leading from the right. Bedding, crockery, cutlery and all the general paraphernalia of living was provided, the sheets were changed once a week, and I arranged for the owner to shift the dust from Point A to Point B three times a week.

I was lucky. As time went by, I gradually realised just how lucky.

Doing nothing can become a full-time occupation. I proved that, as the days grew into weeks and the weeks mounted. It was a good summer, and mid-morning usually saw me strolling past Hesketh Park and towards Marine Drive. A lunch at one of the neat cafés of Lord Street, then an afternoon dozing in the sun in Victoria Park or Princes Park.

I grew slothful. My responsibilities were nil, and I lived from day to day. The thought of Anne's murder dwindled into little more than an annoying irritation of my mind and the warmth of those summer days seemed to draw out the hatred which had previously driven me. To say I was happy would be an over-simplification. I was neither happy nor sad. I was just *there*. While the sun shone I was content. When the showers came I sought shelter at a bar or in an arcade. I dined, as I had lunched, in a café and, each evening, I walked slowly back to my flat without thought of even the next day.

In retrospect it was a mad and very limited life-style, but it suited my mood of the moment and that sufficed.

Meanwhile (and quite naturally) the relationship between my elderly landlady and myself had moved from a 'Mr Ryder' politeness to a 'Charles' familiarity. She wasn't nosey. She accepted my monthly cheque with a smile and a bobbed head and, sometime in early September, took it while she held a cup of tea in her other hand.

'Going to make yourself some supper, Charles?' she asked.

'Something like that.' I nodded at the cup. 'Something warm, before I turn in.'

'Want some? There's enough for two.'

It seemed a good idea and I accepted the invitation.

The first feeling was one of surprise. This old she-bag had money or, if not money, wealth. I was no connoisseur, but even I could see that the furniture wasn't chain-store junk and, at a guess, it was hand-made and probably museum-rare. It needed beeswax and elbow grease, but the class showed through. As with the soft-furnishings, the crockery, the miniatures . . . everything in fact.

So with the talk. Not gossip, but conversation, and she could hold her own. Books; she was the only person I've ever met who's read (and understood) *War And Peace*. Even Proust – and in the original French – came within her ambit. Me? I was only halfway there in the Scott Moncrieff translation.

The same with music. The same with the performing

arts, sculpture and painting. Externally she was salmon-tin silver, but inside she was pure gold.

Gradually, and as the days shortened, it became a habit. Tea and scones or biscuits with her before I retired. And talk. Good talk; talk with body and purpose.

She invited me to an evening meal on Thursday, November the 5th.

Bonfire Night. That's how I remember the date. Her son was visiting her from London, and she wanted us to meet. It seemed okay. Indeed, it seemed a nice idea; if his company was as good as his mother's there was every prospect of an interesting evening.

She called him Sonny, therefore I called him Sonny. Whether that was his real name or an endearing corruption of the word 'son' I never discovered. He was about my age, give or take a few years, presentable, well-dressed and able to hold his own in the chit-chat stakes. It would be unfair to use the expression 'all British male', partly because there's no such animal and partly because he was too friendly, too extrovert, to deserve that description. Nevertheless, physically, that was the immediate impression he gave.

The conversational ball was passed around throughout the meal; then, when the old lady had removed the plates and such, Sonny wandered to the drinks cabinet, poured three brandies and, as he walked back said, very casually, 'A prolonged holiday, Charles?'

'What?'

'Here – at Southport. I'm told you've been here since June.'

'Er – yes – since June.'

'At least since June.' He handed me a drink, and settled into an easy chair.

'Since June,' I repeated.

'What is it?' He smiled, tasted the brandy, then added, 'Not the proceeds from the bank robbery. Bill Wilkinson

75

assures me you weren't part of it.'

It was rather like being kicked in the crotch. Suddenly and very unexpectedly. I even caught my breath and for a moment couldn't speak.

Calmly – even politely – he said, 'You *are* the same Charles Ryder, of course?'

I found myself nodding. What else? Every card in my hand was being trumped, and this Sonny character showed complete unconcern.

'Pendlebridge, wasn't it?' He sipped his drink, again. 'Bill said it was Pendlebridge . . . the last time he contacted you, you were at Pendlebridge.'

'Are you . . .' I swallowed, but couldn't quite moisten my throat. 'Are you the police?'

'Good God, no.' He gave a quick, silent chuckle. 'Not the *police*.'

'What then?'

'A friend of Bill's.' He nodded. 'Drink your brandy, Charles. You're with friends.'

'Friends?'

'Friends of yours . . . acquaintances of Bill's.'

'Relax, Charles.' The woman had joined us. She parked herself in an empty chair, smiled her friendship, and added, 'Sonny's right. You've nothing to worry about.'

'You – you know Bill?' I was gradually regaining my balance.

'*Of* him. Not intimately.' Again the cheerful smile. 'We're – what you might say – in the same line of business . . . more or less.'

' "We"?'

He glanced round the room. 'She didn't have it left, Charles. She bought it.'

'All of it,' she added gently.

'It pays, Charles. It's very lucrative.'

'You mean . . .'

'Don't give it a name, Charles. It's not polite.'

'Like – like Bill?' I choked.

'Bigger than Bill . . . but *like* Bill.'

In a distinctly motherly tone, she said, 'Drink your brandy, Charles. You've had a shock, but you'll get over it.'

He might have been her son. He just *might*. But I doubt it. The only thing I'm sure about is that the next couple of hours were quite unreal. They belonged to a dream, but they *weren't* a dream.

And yet, with hindsight . . .

I'd thought I was hiding, but in fact I'd made myself very obvious.

'For almost six months, Charles. Rich people take holidays as long as that, but rich people don't live in flats like this. Not unemployed – not even retired – you couldn't afford it, or you wouldn't have rented it on a monthly basis. Something else. On the run? That was a possibility worth investigating.'

I hadn't even changed my name.

'Such a silly mistake to make, Charles. Silly for you, fortunate for us. We just asked around. Sent out feelers. It was absurdly simple. Your name. Your description. We identified you weeks ago. Months ago. We were sure. All we needed was verification.'

Stupidity, plus bad luck. *My* bad luck.

'We'd have found you, of course. You or somebody like you. I can tell you now. At first we didn't believe we could be so fortunate. We thought *you* were a plant. It took us weeks to convince ourselves.'

I was into my third large brandy. Well into it. I think I was ever so slightly tipsy; not drunk, but warm and a little numb. I know I gradually didn't care too much any more. I was up a blind alley . . . so what the hell?

Nevertheless, and in my own half-hearted way, I fought back.

I fumbled shredded tobacco into my pipe and said, 'I could blow.'

'Where?'

'Out of here. Somewhere. Anywhere.'

'You think we'd let you?'

'I may be dumb . . .'

'A little.'

'. . . but I can't see how you can stop me.'

'We found you.' He tossed a lighter onto my lap. 'We don't have that problem any more, Charles. We only have to follow you.'

'As easy as that?' I thumbed the lighter and held the flame to the surface of the tobacco.

'Charles,' he said mildly, 'you've been followed for weeks. Months. The cafés, the boozers . . . everywhere. You don't believe me? I'll phone, and give you a run-down on where you've eaten and *what* you've eaten. We don't make mistakes. We can't afford to.'

Almost tenderly, the woman said, 'Where would you go, Charles?'

'Nowhere.' I muttered the word past the stem of my pipe. 'I've run far enough. I'm licked.'

Equally gently, Sonny murmured, 'There's also the matter of your wife. Something the police would like to see you about.'

I nodded, and the movement was a complete and utter capitulation.

I went to bed more drunk than sober, but sober enough to know I was in a rat-trap from which there was no obvious escape. Nor, come to that and deep down inside, had I any real urge to escape. They'd given nothing away. Not really. 'Bigger than Bill . . . but *like* Bill.' What the hell did that mean? Bigger than £200,000. That made them big. Very big! And – or so it seemed – I was earmarked for . . .

For what?

Dammit, they'd given nothing away. Nothing! Even without Anne's murder, I couldn't have touched them. I was tied up in pink ribbon. *With* Anne's murder I was signed, sealed and delivered. What the hell they had in mind I was in it, somewhere. Somewhere.

Okay, the holier-than-thou crowd will tut-tut and say I was gutless. The whiter-than-white jerks. All those prissy people who know exactly how to say 'No' on other people's behalf. But let me remind you.

In all this prolonged, wide-screen mulligatawny, *I had not once stepped out of line*. I was no bank-robber. I was no wife-killer. Nothing. You understand . . . nothing! But for doing 'nothing' I'd lost my job, my marriage had folded, my kids had only contempt for me and the cops couldn't wait to nail me for a murder I knew damn-all about. Plus the fact that I'd been on the run for months.

Okay, I'd smacked Smith in the face with my skull. Okay, I'd accepted £5,000 of dirty money from Bill Wilkinson. And, okay, I'd left Tim and Judy to fend for themselves.

But self-preservation had its price. All I'd done was pay it.

I tried to shower myself more sober, but the more sober I became the more convinced I became. The 'goodies' were bastards. Smith, Anne, the kids, Masters . . . all self-satisfied bastards, who didn't give a damn. The 'baddies'? Bill Wilkinson, Tommy Kelly and his family. They'd given me kindness. They'd given me friendship. Damn it all, they'd *believed*.

So as I climbed into bed the decision was reached.

The hell with the angels . . . I'd try the other side.

I paid no more rent for the flat. I tried, but the old girl wouldn't take it.

'Let's say you're part of the family, Charles.'

I didn't press the matter. I was prepared to make the ride as easy for myself as possible. I stayed in more. Visited the cinema a few times. Waited for something to happen, knowing that it would happen. And having reached the decision, it never entered my mind to take off. I was part of something and when they wanted me to know – whoever 'they' were – I'd be told what that 'something' was.

Meanwhile, and about a week after I'd offered the rent, I checked my current account with the bank. It had grown. It was a few hundred pounds more than it should have been. I was on somebody's payroll, and I wasn't going to be allowed to starve.

'You have a job, Charles.'

I know the date because, as of that evening, I started a diary of sorts. It was Sunday, December the 13th; the 51st Sunday of the year and the 3rd Sunday in Advent. The shops had been full of Christmas sparkle for some time. That Yuletide feel was in the air. 'Messiah' season, goodwill to all men and screw the sheep, get those shepherds geared up and ready for the manger visit.

I'd called in for my evening cuppa and she'd pushed the bulky envelope across the table towards me.

'You have a job, Charles.'

'Really?'

I picked up the envelope and ripped it open as we talked.

'Bills of Lading. Know what they are?'

'Uhuh. They list the cargo carried by ships.'

'Your job is to check them. They've been checked once. Yours is a sort of double-check.'

'Interesting.' I shuffled the various documents around.

'Boring,' she smiled. 'You'll not find any mistakes, but we need you there.'

' "There"?'

'Liverpool.'

'Liverpool?'

'The pass will get you anywhere on the docks. Nobody's your boss. That's been taken care of. Just get there in the morning and come back at night. Go through the motions, but make it look as real as possible.'

'And?'

'That's all. Let them get used to you. Be friendly . . . with everybody.'

'Everybody,' I murmured. 'But specifically?'

'Everybody,' she repeated. 'We don't make mistakes, Charles. Give a name, you'll concentrate on him. Or her. Not deliberately. I'm not saying that. But without realising it. *Don't* give you a name . . . you'll concentrate on everybody. That's what we want. Just don't make enemies.'

'It might be the wrong person.'

'Exactly.' She nodded at the documents I was holding. 'The car. It's yours. On loan for the time being. A Y-registration Polo. Driving licence, insurance . . . everything. It's parked at the back. The ignition key will be on the hall table. Just collect it and go to work.'

'So easy?'

If there was mild mockery in my tone it was a cover-up The butterflies were there in my guts.

Very solemnly she said, 'Charles, you're in the top league. You've seen them. In sport, in acting, in writing. To them, it *is* easy. They don't make mistakes, because they don't go in guyed up with blind faith. They've thought it all out. They know where the mistakes might come and, as far as possible, they've eliminated the likelihood. Like us. Step at a time, Charles. Have patience . . . you'll be a rich man.'

A motor car and enough documentation to dump me back among the human race. Driving Licence. Certificate of Insurance. National Insurance Card. Vehicle Registration Document. All stamped and signed with what even *I* would have taken for a genuine signature. Nor were we tooling around with false names; names which might cause a trip-up at the wrong moment. The beard. The fuller face. I was still Charles Ryder, and could prove it up to the hilt. But I was *another* Charles Ryder.

And that pass to the docks was like magic.

The security man on the gate checked it against a form

81

fastened to a clipboard, touched the peak of his cap and said, 'Ah yes, Mr Ryder. First day here, sir. I'll show you how to get to the office you work out of.'

And at the office.

'Ryder . . . good to have you. Take your time. Get used to things. Then when you're ready, these Bills of Lading. You'll find the craft moored next to the Elder Dempster tub, along the wharf.'

The ground had been well prepared. But who was and who wasn't? Innocents were caught up in the net. That for sure. In fact most, if not all, were innocent. That or the whole damn dock force was in the swindle . . . and that wasn't possible. Therefore, who? Or (and as far as I could see it was quite possible) had this mysterious organisation of which I was now a part enough pull to influence the *real* masters, who never even visited the docks?

Figuratively speaking, I lay back and thought of England. Or, if not of England, of Charles Ryder.

I used that near-fortnight before Christmas to acquaint myself with the docks, the wharves, the loading bays, the warehouses and even the custom sheds . . . and not once was that pass questioned.

I drove back to Southport that Christmas Eve, and Yorkshire pulled like the devil. I yearned for the white rose acres, my home county, and the hell with Southport or anything west of the Pennines, south of the Humber or north of Staithes. I wanted 'home'. *My* home. The home every Yorkshireman worth his salt carries locked away in his heart.

Could be the tension was mounting. I wouldn't argue. Like quicksands, every time I moved I seemed to get deeper in, and that had been happening for a long time. Could be *that*, but I didn't think so. Just Yorkshire and, if explanations are necessary, you'll never understand. That's what I figured.

Back at the flat I tackled the old lady.

I said, 'I thought a break. A Christmas break. I have until a week Monday. I thought a short holiday.'

'Where?'

The question carried curiosity, but I didn't detect suspicion.

'Yorkshire. It's where I belong.'

'Haggthorpe?'

'God, no. Not Haggthorpe. I'm not *that* crazy.'

'Where, Charles?'

'I thought the Dales. Maybe the Dales. Maybe the coast.'

'Nowhere in particular?' she smiled.

'Nowhere in particular,' I agreed. 'Just take the car and travel. Be back here next weekend. Saturday, Sunday, I'd let you know.'

'A strange way to spend Christmas, Charles.'

'Hell, I haven't a home.'

'This is your home.'

'No. I just live here. I'm not complaining . . . but it's not home.'

A tiny frown creased the space between and above her eyes.

'Nothing foolish, Charles,' she said gently.

'I'll be back,' I promised.

'Money?'

'I have my cheque book.'

'No.' She shook her head. 'That stays. And your banker's card. *And* your driving licence, insurance, registration certificate. Basic precautions, Charles. It's not that we don't trust you . . . we *can't* trust anybody.'

'I'll need money.'

'Two hundred pounds?'

'Look, if I'd wanted to take off, I'd have been able . . .'

'On the other hand, Charles, you *might* be being very cunning. A week – at least a week – of absolute freedom.'

'No.'

'We can't chance it, Charles.'

'Okay,' I sighed. 'Two hundred pounds.'

'Two-fifty.' She smiled. That innocent, maternal smile that meant damn-all. 'It's Christmas, Charles. You might want to buy somebody a present.'

Later that evening I set off and, before closing time, I'd booked in at Ripon Spa Hotel and was standing at the bar, enjoying a quiet drink and wallowing in seasonal friendship with happy strangers.

It was a good idea. The best idea I'd had for years. I hadn't counted on it, but the Dales were curiously quiet throughout the Christmas period. It wasn't the tourist season, and visitors were rare. Yet the food was magnificent and the comfort out of this world. A homely comfort. More than that, even. The dalesfolk knew how to celebrate Christmas; knew what good grub and good booze boiled down to. Nothing fancy. Nothing continental. Turkey, pork and beef, oven-cooked, done to a turn and sliced thick. Fresh vegetables, garden- or greenhouse-grown. Plum pudding, tangy with rum and swimming in smooth white sauce. And mince pies, warm and mouth-watering. Then real ale or good malt whisky.

And after the gorging, a snooze in the enveloping warmth of a real fire. Coal or log, it didn't matter. The flames curled and spat and the heat was primaeval and not from a glowing bar or warm air; good heat, honest heat and something you knew was as alive as you were.

And friendship. Not shallow friendship. Fleeting, perhaps, but with a depth which, while it was there, left no room for doubt.

God, I enjoyed that Christmas week!

Saturday saw me at the Devonshire Hotel in Grassington. A Dales pub with a name like that . . . *and* looking out onto the square of this overtly Yorkshire township. But the locals liked it (as, indeed, did I) and forgave it its southern name.

I stayed there Sunday night, too, then moved on to Settle and the Golden Lion.

Another fine pub, with breath-taking views from its windows. Again loved by the locals . . . and with reason. That was Monday. So-called 'Innocents' Day'. That night there was a new moon, and I saw it from my bedroom window. A silver thread like a razor-nick in the star-scattered sky. Any muck – any hint of industrial smog – and it wouldn't have been visible, but there it was, as innocent as the year fast approaching.

That, I think, is one reason why that December break was so memorable. The year was ending and it had been one hell of a year. Twelve months back I'd had just about everything. Now? Even simple freedom had to be paid for.

Maybe the new year would bring , . .

I couldn't even name it, but whatever it was . . . maybe.

On the Tuesday I drove along minor and unclassified roads. No destination. No particular direction. I've thought about it since. Could be I was looking for Tommy. Not deliberately, but sub-consciously. As I recall I didn't even think of him, but the mind shoots off on journeys of its own; it sometimes doesn't even tell you; it wanders away, then returns, without you being aware that it was gone. Therefore, could be. I'd had great happiness with the Kelly family. I'd had a contentment I hadn't known previously, nor had known since. And, in some cheap romantic novel I would, no doubt, have found Tommy, there'd have been a great and tearful reunion and, thereafter, happy ever more.

But this was real-life. I didn't find Tommy. I didn't even knowingly look for him.

But I found a farmhouse. God knows where it was. I couldn't find it again. The legend 'B & B' had been burned into a board nailed to the gate, and dusk was only a couple of hours away. It invited, and I accepted the invitation.

The farmer's father-in-law made the next few hours unforgettable.

Having been accepted, been shown my bedroom and then been placed in a comfortable chair before the near-obligatory furnace-like fire, the old chap opened the conversation with a blunt question.

'Have you eaten?' (Actually, he said, 'As tha et'n ?' but, for the sake of understanding and sanity, I must translate Dalesman's Yorkshire into moderate English.)

I admitted that, other than a snack lunch after a massive breakfast, I had not eaten.

'Nay, lad.' He leaned sideways in his chair and bawled through the open door leading into the farmhouse kitchen. 'Hey, Mabel. There's a chap here faint from lack of nourishment.'

Then it came. Home-baked bread, home-churned butter, home-made chutney and a dinner-plate-sized slice of home-cured, home-boiled ham almost a quarter-of-an-inch thick. Tea, strong and sweet and served in a pint beaker, with the tea-pot placed on the hearth ready for re-filling.

Who *can't* feel hungry when faced with that?

And (but of course) the old chap joined me, and had the same.

Beyond the boundaries of Yorkshire – indeed beyond the confines of the Dales – people would have had difficulty in understanding him. But I understood him and enjoyed the broad vowels and the clipped or missing consonants with the pleasure of a music-lover hearing a Beethoven symphony after having been starved of music for years. And he could talk. He openly admitted it.

'They tell me I can yack a bit.'

I answered his questions, but kept my answers short. I wanted to listen to *him*; to flavour the joy of genuine Dalesman dialect spoken by a man who knew no other way of talking. Blunt to the point of near-rudeness, but accompanied by a ready chuckle which robbed the words of offence.

'Where do you say you're from?

'Southport? That's a very hoity-toity place, so they tell me.

'How is it you're not home for Christmas?

'Nay, everybody's got a home, lad. Somewhere.

'Well, I'm right sorry for you, lad. You want to get yourself married. Settle down and make a home for yourself.

'Where do you say you work?

'Liverpool? That's a muck-hole, so they tell me.'

Then, when the four of us were sitting in a semi-circle around the fire, with the Christmas cards almost jostling each other from the mantelshelf and the record-player softly playing King's College carols in the background, 'Right. Let's have a bit of a drink. A drop of home-brewed stuff.'

Then it came. Elderflower wine. Parsnip wine. Wheat wine. Each with its own subtle flavour. Each as gentle as a mother's kiss, but with a delayed kick like an enraged cart-horse. We drank it from tumblers – half-tumbler at a time – and they had to help me up the stairs to the bedroom.

But no hang-over.

After the gargantuan breakfast, I tried to pay for the evening meal and the added hospitality, but they would have none of it. The old chap was almost offended.

'You've been good company, lad. Not like some bloodless buggers we get.'

And that was it. I even forget their name, but I'll never forget *them*. I'll never forget *him*.

On the Wednesday I drove east from the Dales, and by early afternoon was talking to Bill Wilkinson.

Why?

Anybody can be wise after the event and indulge in parlour psychology. That whole Christmas period can be 'explained' in fancy language and high-flown terms of art.

The truth is, I don't know. Those few hours at the farm, and the unqualified friendship? The undoubted fact that, since leaving the Kelly family, I hadn't *had* a friend? Equally, the way I'd lived my whole life, and the gradual realisation that I'd collected so *few* friends? Dammit, it was Christmas. I hadn't a family. I wanted *somebody*.

Whatever the reason, I telephoned and insisted that he join me, if only for a few hours.

He was awkward. That much had been obvious on the telephone. Nevertheless, he'd agreed to meet me in a Harrogate restaurant, and he met me . . . and was still awkward. Uncomfortable. Nervous.

I watched him, as we sipped coffee and nibbled cheese and biscuits. He was watching people. Not the same self-assured Bill. Suspicious. Maybe even frightened.

'Have you been up to something, Bill?' I asked.

'What?' He almost jumped at the question.

'For God's sake! I'm not . . .'

'No. Nothing. We took enough with the last job.'

'It's just that . . .'

'Don't ask, Charles. Don't ask.'

'What?'

'Nothing.' He moistened his lips. 'Let's talk, Charles. By all means let's talk. But not about each other . . . right?'

'You mean Smith's been . . .'

'*Don't!*' The soft plea had terror at its core. He almost groaned, 'Not about each other, Charles. Anything – football, boozing, birds – anything, but not about each other.'

'Okay, okay,' I soothed. 'Pick a subject.'

Which is why what we said was as meaningless as a TV chat-show. Conversational garbage grubbed around in by strangers. It added up to damn-all. I had this stupid feeling. That I was talking to Bill . . . but Bill wasn't *there*. I was wasting part of my life and in doing so, screwing up my end-of-year holiday.

What had I expected?

I don't know. Friendship? Certainly friendship, but if friendship was there it was being choked by something well beyond my comprehension. A few laughs, perhaps? It wasn't asking too much. Not from Bill. Not from the Bill I'd once known *That* Bill had been fundamentally decent and hadn't given a toss for anybody. But *this* Bill . . .

Sure, sure, I'd asked him to meet an on-the-run murder suspect, and Smith was a bastard on all points of the compass. Maybe I'd put him at risk. Maybe Smith and his minions had given him hell; had squeezed all the juice from him; had used him for too long as the only link they had with me. Maybe that and, if so, I was sorry.

Whatever, it was a lousy few hours. He was obviously glad to go, and the truth is *I* wasn't sorry either.

By Wednesday evening I was back in the Dales and bedded up at the Palmer Flatt Hotel at Aysgarth. Another nice pub, within spitting distance of Aysgarth Falls. A tourist spot. One of *the* tourist spots of the Dales, but that night I saw no tourists. Locals filled the rustic bar and the season was in full swing, but that night mine was the only one of the fifteen bedrooms occupied. It was a pity. It was beautiful . . . and that is the only word with which to describe the magnificent solitude which surrounded us. I opened my bedroom window and heard the rush of the falls, and that sound with its soft background of wildlife noises reflected my thoughts. Sadness, perhaps. Maybe a hint of self-pity. But above all, loneliness. The loneliness of nature and the wild creatures. And peace, of course. That brand of peace which tends to choke a little.

I need not have been alone. I've thought of that, too. Without too much effort, I could have had a companion. A woman. No . . . a lady. Not a tart. Not a pick-up. A bed-companion who might, or might not, have added to my pleasure. There are too many good, but lonely, people around for it to have been difficult. I need not have been alone.

I was, however, and it was by choice. Not conscious choice, perhaps, but a choice determined by the facts of the year just coming to a close.

Anne had hurt me. She was dead and God rest her soul, but she *had* hurt me. More than I'd been able to tell her. Probably more than she'd realised. A wrongly-accused man, I'd come from the court wanting and expecting sympathy. If from nobody else, from her. But she'd let me down. In effect she'd believed Smith and, in so doing, had called me a liar. Indeed, she *had* called me a liar. *And* a thief. She'd toppled my world and, however hard I'd tried, it had remained toppled.

And after that . . .

Women were not to be trusted. Correction . . . *my* women were not to be trusted. Those who *could* be trusted – like Seonad – already had their men. The game wasn't worth the candle. I could do without women. I could do without sex. I was a big boy now.

Okay, cynicism – self-pity – childishness – a dozen and more other things, but I didn't *need* a woman.

On the Thursday I moved into Swaledale. To Grinton and the Bridge Hotel. This time moors and a stretch of the river and peace which, to me, wasn't quite the peace I was seeking, and a breeze which sliced like hot steel and – why shouldn't I admit it? – a handful of lonely tears I couldn't hold back. A nice place; as nice as all the others. Fine food; I was eating better than I'd eaten in all my life. Good company; without that black imp squatting on my shoulder I could have been deep-down happy with all the people I met, but I was honest enough to recognise superficial happiness when I experienced it. So, I stayed at the Bridge the night, sang Auld Lang Syne with the real revellers, rang Southport, wished the old crone a Happy New Year and told her to expect me back on the Friday, then tried to drink myself unconscious.

No way!

The Pacific couldn't have drowned my mood.

Friday, January the 8th . . .

That was the day I learned a lesson. The day I finally *realised*.

The day had been only moderately boring; I'd carried Bills of Lading around, exchanged empty talk with a handful of people, swallowed a few pints of tea and chewed my way through a few sandwiches and generally done damn-all to earn my pay. I'd garaged the car and was entering the house when the door to the old lady's apartments opened and she greeted me.

'Charles, have you a few minutes?'

'Sure.'

'You like trout?'

'Trout?'

'Rainbow trout. We're having it. I've laid three places.'

'We?'

'Sonny's come up to see me. He'd like a word.'

'Oh!'

'If you can spare the time.'

She was being polite, not sarcastic. Nor was it a put-on. I'd already come to accept that truth; that these bastards *didn't* think they were bent. They ran a tightly organised business. Like Bill . . . but *bigger* than Bill. That was their own description of how they came to have more money than anybody else I knew; money with which the old lady bought class furniture; money with which they'd handed me a steady income for doing sweet F.A.; money with which they'd bought me a brand new personality. That size of purse, and that was only part of it. It could only be a *part* of it.

Therefore, she was being polite. She was not being

91

sarcastic.

So, I enjoyed trout for that evening meal. Grilled trout with all the trimmings and accompanied by gentle, educated conversation. Sonny was pleasant, the old lady was pleasant, nobody put a foot wrong or said a mischievous word.

I was sitting in my usual armchair, enjoying a steady-drawing pipe, when the nitty-gritty started to show. But still quietly. Still amicably. Still without any obvious threat.

'Nice break, Charles?' Sonny turned the ash from his cigarette into an ash-tray as he asked the question.

'You mean Christmas-New Year?'

'Uhuh. Enjoy it?'

'Pleasant,' I admitted. 'Very pleasant.'

'Where?'

'The Dales.'

'Beautiful.' He drew on the cigarette. 'A little commercialised these days, but beautiful.'

'I think so.'

'Haggthorpe?'

'Would I be so foolish?' I smiled.

'I don't think so.' He returned the smile, then asked, 'Harrogate?'

'I called.'

'Yeah . . . Bill told us.'

'Bill? Bill Wilkinson?'

'He told us you'd met him in Harrogate. A meal, he said.'

'Yeah. A meal of sorts.'

'Enjoy it?'

'What?'

'The meal.'

'So-so.' I moved my shoulders. 'I ate better meals.'

'In the Dales?'

'Good grub.' I pulled a little harder on my pipe. I thought it was going out on me. 'Couldn't be bettered.'

'Yorkshire fare?'

'That's what it boils down to.'

As he drew on his cigarette, the old lady said, 'What did you talk about, Charles?'

'Talk about?'

'To Bill Wilkinson.'

'This and that.' I waved the stem of my pipe airily.

'What's "this"? What's "that"?' asked Sonny, gently.

'What the hell . . .'

'Try to remember, Charles.'

'Nothing important.' They were starting to get under my skin. My tone tended to show it. 'The hell, it's almost a week since. It's . . .'

'More than a week since, Charles,' she interrupted.

'Eh?'

Sonny murmured, 'Nine days ago, Charles. Wednesday the thirtieth. In the afternoon.'

'In that case . . .'

'Charles, don't be difficult. What did you talk about?' She added, 'What *did* you talk about, Charles?'

'Your new job?' he asked.

'No. Why should I . . .'

'Liverpool?'

'No.'

'This place?'

'No.'

'The docks?'

'God damn it, no.'

'Us?'

'Why the hell should I . . .'

'Charles, did you mention Liverpool? Did you mention the docks? Did you mention Southport? This place? Did you mention us?'

'Hell's teeth . . . *no!*'

I was almost shouting. Sonny wasn't. As I grew louder, he grew softer, and that gave him the overtaking lane. I retained enough sense to realise that and I quietened myself. It took an effort, but I made it.

In a more reasonable voice, I said, 'We talked about nothing. The sort of talk you forget within minutes of parting. He didn't even want to talk.'

'No?'

'Didn't want to listen. He was scared ... about something.'

'Did he say what he was scared of?'

'No. He wouldn't tell me.' I scraped a match and held the flame to the burned tobacco. I continued speaking around the stem of my pipe. 'Had I wanted to, what the hell could I have told him? I don't know a thing.'

The old lady shook her head and said, 'You know too much, Charles.'

'Okay.' I waved the match out. 'That's what you tell me. It's not important. I didn't tell Bill anything.'

'I hope not,' said Sonny, mildly.

'Ask Bill.'

'We've asked him. That's what *he* said.'

'You've been in touch?'

'He telephoned us. Told us. We met him, and asked him.'

'So, what's the beef?' I blew a plume of smoke. 'Ring him again. Double-check.'

She said, 'We can't do that, Charles.'

'Why not? You have his . . .'

'He's dead.' Sonny used a flat, expressionless tone. Not loud. Just flat. 'He fell out of a top-floor window.'

'He . . .' That was as far as I got before my jaw dropped and my mouth opened.

'Fortunately.' The same flat tone. Saying one thing, but meaning another. 'The day we asked him. He didn't know, but he might have guessed.'

I took it like a man. I fool not one hair's breadth; I closed my mouth, froze my muscles, controlled my breathing and took it. A lot of it was natural self-preservation but (I hope) some of it was for the sake of a very nice guy whose hobby had been armed robbery.

For the moment, I didn't even think about it.

The talk moved on, from murder to other things. More important things. Things like modern jazz. Dammit, I *remember*. Oscar Peterson was doing a one-nighter at Southport early in the year, and we solemnly chewed over the old Oscar Peterson/Art Tatum argument.

But not later. Not when I'd moved up into my own flat.

That's when the shakes got me.

I stood under a steaming shower, but I still trembled. I changed into pyjamas and dressing-gown, put the gas fire on at full and slurped neat whisky, but it was no good. That block of ice in my guts refused to melt.

'He might have guessed.' Big deal! Whatever fancy calculations Bill might have come up with would have been based upon something I'd told him. Something I *knew*. So, if he'd been capable of guessing, where did that leave me?

Not to duck the issue, it left me half-way out of a high-storey window.

Suddenly, and by comparison, Smith became a bosom friend.

No other cop. In the first place I didn't know any other cops, and it was too late to strike up an acquaintance. Also, Smith was a past-master at playing with bees in his bonnet. Also, Smith wanted me; he was crazy to get his hands on me. Boy! He could *have* me. He could have me all the way down to the underpants, just let him dump me somewhere where the pigeons couldn't crap on me, and for as long as possible.

That was how I felt the night I heard of Bill Wilkinson's death. A state of mind warranted to bring on bad dreams and, when I slept, I had bad dreams.

At that time, and despite everything, I did damn-all.

Dawn brought false logic. What if I *did* know things I

shouldn't know? Things I didn't even *know* I knew? Whatever their scheme was, and whoever 'they' were, I was a part of the picture. I'd already cost them too much for them to hoik *me* from a window. They wanted me alive and active. Out there on the docks, being buddy-buddy with everybody.

Okay . . . so be it. I'd play along; play at being patsy, but keep my nerve-ends twitching. Something big was on the way, and getting closer. Give it time. Let things ease themselves forward at *their* pace. Me? All I was doing was wandering around with Bills of Lading in my hand. Nothing naughty in that. Nothing even suspicious. So lead them up the garden path Ryder, my friend, but draw an invisible chalk-line and when they step across that line – when they *really* drop their breeks and expose themselves – *then* start blowing whistles.

It is known as not being wise. It is known as being naive. It is also known as being bloody stupid.

Nevertheless, February elbowed January aside, and the wind blew snow across the Mersey, and the sheds and warehouses formed canyons along which gale-force blasts threatened to take the flesh from your face. But it was healthy and I liked it, and I grew to know people.

There is about Merseyside something unique. Maybe it's the water. Maybe it's the air. Whatever it is, it is magic. Count them. The artists, the writers, the sculptors, the playwrights, the actors and the actresses. To say nothing of the musicians and the comedians. The Beatles were spawned there, and The Beatles are only a peak in a large and impressive range. As for the comics. It seems that every alternate funny man was born a Scouse . . . and, having worked with them, I know why.

Liverpool is a city which at first glance is all slum, and in parts a slum *of* a slum. And yet, they laugh; they see humour in a forced life-style whose average makes simple poverty seem plenty. They make a joke about living conditions a Russian peasant wouldn't tolerate. They honestly don't give a damn, because to give a damn would mean dying of a broken heart. Therefore they stay, laugh at it, then work like hell to get out . . . and, having got out, they can joke about *anything*.

I met and worked alongside men from that city. Men who refused to be broken. Men whose drollery boiled down to a spit in the eye of crazy bureaucracy. They thieved, they twisted, they swindled and, as they did so, they gagged and chuckled. Nothing was sacred, nothing was serious. Everything was bent, buggered or barred. Therefore if they wanted something, they helped themselves, but when they worked (which was long and often) they grafted.

The dockers, for example. They feared nothing on two legs or four. Time and again I watched them put their lives at risk in order to cut corners and load, or unload, some vessel on time. Hard drinking, hard swearing men; pot-bellied, steel-muscled and fearsome when aroused. They knew what they were – the pores through which the nation breathed – and they refused to sell themselves short.

I grew to love them, but at the same time, I watched them. Man at a time I evaluated their possible basic honesty. Which was the one? Which was the one Sonny had in his pocket? Which, of these fantastic men, could somebody like the old lady – could *anybody* – bribe or frighten into submission?

I was wrong. I discovered exactly how wrong on the evening of Sunday, February the 28th. The last day of the month.

It had been a bad day. An east wind and snow flurries; the sort of weather that has the windows rattling. I'd mushed myself scrambled egg for breakfast, ventured out for a Sunday newspaper, brought back a takeaway pack for lunch and spent the afternoon mulling through the flash

97

crap of the Sunday supplement. I was toying with the idea of smartening myself up and having dinner at the Prince of Wales when the knock came on the door, and the old lady invited me down for an evening meal.

I sensed it. Not from what she said, and it wasn't the first time she'd asked me down, but at the back of her eye there was that extra, barely-noticeable gleam. But I'd come to look for it and I saw it, so I wasn't surprised to find Sonny sprawled out, waiting.

The usual pattern. The meal – genuine Lancashire hot-pot and when it's done well and by an expert hot-pot is a *very* tasty dish – then a relaxation in armchairs, pending the old lady moving the dirty crocks. A pipe, cigarettes, a drink. Friendly conviviality, pending the gentle dropping of the boom. I'd come to expect it, and it didn't catch me one-footed any more. I was shockproof.

Very casually, Sonny said, 'Tiny.'

I grunted, and waited for it.

'Know him?'

'One of the security guards.'

'How well do you know him, Charles?' she asked.

'So-so. We pass the time of day.'

'No arguments? No differences of opinion?' Sonny drew on his cigarette. 'Nothing like that?'

'Those weren't my instructions,' I reminded him.

'True.' He smiled. 'How much do you know about him, Charles?'

'He's a security guard. Pleasant enough. I think he's divorced. He . . .'

'He's a widower,' he chipped in gently. 'He has a daughter. A teenager. He's a jazz-buff.' He slipped an envelope from an inside pocket and held it out. 'Four tickets for Blackpool Winter Gardens. Sunday, April the eighteenth. A one-stop concert by the Lionel Hampton outfit.'

'Know him, Charles?' she asked.

'Tiny?'

'No . . . Lionel Hampton.'

'Of him. About him. I don't know him, personally.'

'Mug up on him,' said Sonny quietly.

'I don't have to. I know my jazz.'

'Nevertheless . . .' He waved the cigarette airily. 'This Tiny character knows his onions. Be able to meet him in the enthusiasm stakes. Get near him. Near enough to be able to treat him to that concert. He's a lonely man. His wife died less than a year ago. He's still dizzy. It shouldn't be too difficult . . . not with jazz as a foundation.'

'Four tickets?' I murmured.

'Four. You don't have to *use* four. You just might *need* four.'

She smiled and added, 'We aren't cheapskates, Charles.'

They'd chosen well. I guessed that when they named him and, as I came to know him, I realised how well.

'Tiny' . . . because he topped the six-two mark in his stocking feet. Broad-shouldered and slim-waisted, he could have been the guy who kicked sand into lesser men's faces, but like so many giants he was too much of a gentleman. His hair was receding a little, and there was a touch of shamble in the way he walked, but he was around thirteen stone of uncomplicated decency. The voice matched the frame. It was a few semi-tones lower than average, but I never heard it raised; had it had a colour and a texture it would have been dark brown velvet.

I began calling in at the office. At first, I invented excuses then, as we grew to know each other, I didn't need excuses. We jelled, and not only because Sonny had arranged that we should jell. He was amazingly easy to be with; given to long, warm silences, punctuated with smiling enthusiasms. Smiling . . . but sad-smiling. As if they'd once been shared enthusiasms which now couldn't be shared and, because of this, he felt some sort of guilt. He was that sort of man; he didn't wear his heart on his sleeve – nothing like that – but the heart was there and it was more than cracked.

And he knew his jazz.

I, too, knew jazz and, as something of a safety-net, I'd borrowed a couple of books from the library to remind myself how much I knew, but alongside Tiny I was a Toc H candle trying to outshine a searchlight.

That first deliberate meeting showed the guide-lines.

Luck was with me, I forget the excuse but I'd visited the office and the tiny transistor was tuned to the local station. The DJ was mouthing the usual moronic nothings while in the background a record of a big band playing *American Patrol* was trying to ease its sound past the conversational garbage. I waited until the drum break had passed before I spoke.

'Not Glenn Miller,' I said, and knew I was right. 'That was *not* Ray McKinley.'

Tiny's eyes gleamed, and he said, 'Joe Loss.'

'McKinley's break,' I said, solemnly. 'If you know it, you can't miss it.'

'Check.'

We grinned at each other, as only aficionados riding their mutual hobby-horse can grin.

'A very under-rated drummer,' I declared.

'Not by those who know. I'd say among the top ten of all time.'

'Better than Pollack?' I made it into a question.

'Big-band-wise.' He nodded.

'Could be. Pollack was a small combo man.'

'McKinley was very solid. He could carry a large orchestra.'

'Could be.' I didn't want to be a Yes-man, but already I knew I was exchanging opinions with a man steeped in a music I, too, loved. I added, 'Like Buddy Rich used to be. Before he turned virtuoso.'

'Krupa was the best,' he said.

'Krupa was the best,' I agreed.

100

That first meeting set the tone. I stopped needing excuses. An exchange of jazz-talk – big band or trad – was excuse enough. We talked of days long-gone; days when musical giants had honed and polished a new kind of music; days when the kids had not been brainwashed into accepting amplified crap as something special. When not to be able to identify Goodman from Shaw, within four bars, showed a sad lack of musical appreciation. Our respective days of salad, when we'd both been happy and in our prime.

It was, I think, the only good thing Sonny or the old lady ever did for me – to make me get to know Tiny - and the bastards didn't *mean* it that way . . . it just happened.

Because it 'happened', I pushed other things to the back of my mind. I'd become a world expert at self-kidology. Black was only black if I looked at it. If I closed my eyes and concentrated, the black disappeared, and all that was left was pure and wholesome. I was a past-master at walking through life with my eyes closed. Dammit, I even fooled myself into believing that I *was* employed checking Bills of Lading.

That's how blind crazy I'd become.

I make no excuses. I only record it as it happened; that I was bad luck to everybody I touched, and that I touched some very nice people.

Sunday, April the 18th . . .

We had a date at Blackpool Winter Gardens, and we were going to see, and listen to, a legend. Just the two of us. Alison, Tiny's daughter, had caught the mood and, although she couldn't understand, she was happy because her father was happy.

'Charles.' She touched my arm while Tiny was out of the room, looked into my face and whispered, 'Thanks.'

I knew what she meant. She was a sweet child. About the

same age as Judy and very wise. That was why she wasn't coming along. Just for one evening – just for a few hours – Tiny could ease memories of his recently-dead wife aside and, hopefully, ride the swing of a man who'd once shared the stage with Goodman and Krupa, James and Wilson. Tiny was like a kid with a new top and, just to be sure, Alison didn't want to be around to stir up the once-upon-a-times.

He'd asked me to his neat semi in Kirkby for a late-afternoon meal and, for almost an hour before we moved off for Blackpool, he played me tapes and records of the old stuff. Ellington and Basie, Berigan and Dorsey, and some of the lesser-known-but-still-great men of the age of jazz; John Kirby, Red Allen and Mezz Mezzrow.

It was a driving, foot-tapping curtain-raiser to an evening we both remembered.

Maybe it was the Hampton vibes. The electric atmosphere created by a theatre solid with the sad-sweet appreciation of a sound from another age. Music can do that. All music; be it classical, big band jazz, chamber, solo or small combination. Only let it be good – the best of its kind – and words become empty vehicles upon which to convey feelings. Music can touch well-springs hitherto not even guessed at . . . and maybe *that* was why.

I pulled into a lay-by, wound down the window, then packed and lighted my pipe. Tiny didn't smoke, and I had no intention of turning the inside of the Polo into a bar-room fug, but it was more than that. I wanted the keyed-up emotion of the last few hours to ease. I also wanted to marshal my thoughts and my words. I was jumping from a ledge. Not perhaps blindfold, in that I thought I knew Tiny well enough to guess his reaction, but nevertheless as much care as possible was called for.

He leaned back in the seat, clasped his fingers behind his neck and sighed, 'A great night, Charles.'

'Superb,' I agreed.

'How in hell people can not like that – at least *like* it – I'll never know.'

I grunted, and allowed the friendly silence time to form some sort of span with which to bridge his happiness and what I was going to say.

Then very quietly – very calmly – I began.

'Tiny, we haven't known each other very long.'

'Long enough.'

'Perhaps. I hope so. Long enough for you to accept what I'm going to say. To believe it.'

'Sure I'll believe it.' I could almost see the warm friendship engendered by the concert leaving him. In the wash of passing headlights I saw the puzzled frown folding his forehead. 'Why shouldn't I believe what you're telling me?'

'I've lied,' I said gently. It was the sort of admission you couldn't cushion. It had to be made and there was no easy way of making it. 'Those tickets tonight. I didn't buy them. I had them given. Four of them . . . that's why the two seats alongside us were empty. I was given them to get close to you, Tiny. I was . . .'

'Hey, what is this?'

'Let me finish, Tiny. It's hard enough to say without being interrupted. Just let me tell you . . . then I'll answer questions.'

He nodded, then kept a stone-faced silence while I told the story. The bank robbery I *hadn't* been part of; the loss of my job; the meeting with Bill Wilkinson; the murder of Anne and my escape from police custody; the flat at Southport (but not the address) and the old lady and Sonny; the con of my job on the docks and the killing of Bill. I worked to keep it as cool as possible. A straight yarn with no frills. I also tried to read his expression in the gloom, but couldn't. But I told it all. I couldn't do less. With a tale like that, it was all or nothing.

I ended, struck a match, put the flame to the half-filled bowl of my pipe and waited.

'So why tell me now?' he asked slowly.

'Call it conscience. Call it friendship.'

'What would *you* call it?'

'A little of both. And I want to get out from under. I've wanted it a long time, but I've lacked the guts. Let's say Lionel Hampton helped.'

'Sure . . . and let's also say all this is an extension of the original come-on.'

'What good would that do?'

'I don't know, Charles. *You* tell *me*.'

'No.' I shook my head. I drew smoke in from the pipe, then said, 'I'm on a limb, Tiny. By telling you I've put myself there and damn near sawn the branch off.'

'I could be one of them. One of Sonny's crowd.'

'That you could,' I agreed solemnly. 'If you *are* I doubt if I'll see any more jazz concerts.'

'As tough as that?'

'Believe me, Tiny. Tough enough to scare the crap out of me.'

He screwed his face up in thought for about two minutes, then nodded slowly, as if he'd reached some sort of a decision.

'Let me sleep on it, Charles.'

'Sure. But – for my sake – don't pass it on.'

'Not until we've had another word,' he promised.

It was all I could expect. Perhaps more than I'd expected. It didn't make much difference . . . it was all I was going to get.

I knocked out my pipe, wound up the window and started the car. Neither of us spoke until we reached Tiny's house in Kirkby, then he made as if to say something, changed his mind and grunted a not-particularly-unfriendly 'Goodnight' and climbed from the car.

And now the boats had all gone up in flames. I'd crossed the river and no way could I turn back.

I drove very slowly back to Southport, garaged the car and climbed the stairs to my flat and, every inch of the way, I worried. Music, you see. It can make you do fine things. It can also make you do very foolish things. Like a drug you can't control. As powerful as any drug and as dangerous . . . and I didn't know.

Accepting that Tiny was all he seemed to be – that he wasn't an involved plant thought up by Sonny and his crowd in order to measure my own reliability – I was still on murderously thin ice. A natural reaction – indeed a proper reaction – would be to tell the port authorities and, if that happened, that was me finished. *Really* finished. Some high window somewhere. Maybe an eight-wheeler in the small of my back one dark night. It could be done. I had no doubts about that. It could be done, and Sonny and his people could arrange it.

Which meant that Tiny had better believe what I'd told him and *everything* I'd told him – not just part of it, not even most of it – because if he didn't believe it *all* . . .

I had a very troubled night.

The next morning it was after eleven before I plucked up enough courage to visit his office. He nodded a civil enough greeting, but people were passing or coming in or going out all the time. I waited, and while I waited we muttered inconsequentialities about the weather and such, but nothing was said about the previous night. I was damn near wetting myself with worry when he said, 'Remember that first day you called in here?'

I nodded.

'The Joe Loss version of *American Patrol*?'

'I remember.'

'There's a Muggsy Spanier recording.'

'Is there? I didn't know.'

'Like to hear it?'

'Yeah . . . I guess.'

I didn't really know what the hell's teeth he was getting at, but I had brains enough to sense that it was something, so I played along.

'Sure you'd like to hear it?'

'Of course.' I nodded. 'I'll say "Please", if that's what you want.'

'No need.' For the first time, something like a smile touched his lips. 'We'll go to my place this evening.'

'Fine.'

And that was me taken care of until the evening. I was nervous throughout the day; watching eyes and wondering whether *they* were watching *me*. A mild and nagging headache was my only companion, and I realised that somebody in that ant's nest of dockers and workers might well be there to keep a check on me. Somebody who knew as little as I and probably less, but whose job it was to report back to either the old lady or somebody deep in the shadows.

Somebody . . . somebody . . . somebody . . .

That was the hell of it. Like rat-droppings. That's all Sonny and the old lady were. The droppings. But because they were there, you knew the rat was around, but you couldn't make any sensible guess as to its size. Just that it was big. Big enough to catch and keep *me* in its jaws, but that was no real measure of its size. The hell, it was big enough to wangle me this job that wasn't a job. It was big enough to pay me and keep me for months; big enough to throw Bill Wilkinson from a window; big enough to take no real heed of a little thing like money.

I thought about it, then tried to stop thinking about it, because the possibilities scared me. It was a little like not being able to swim, treading water and trying to stop yourself from drowning. The panic came up in waves; it tightened your muscles and quivered your nerves; you knew damn well you *had* to relax – that if you *didn't* relax you'd go under – but no way !

* * *

The big, soft, great-hearted man.

I'd followed his car in the Polo; parked and followed him into the house. Alison was out, but she'd left beefburgers and chips ready to be fried. And I'd wanted to talk, but he'd brushed my attempts aside and slipped a cassette into its slot.

'Priorities, Charles. Muggsy Spanier first. Then we eat. *Then* we untie a few knots.'

The food had damn-near choked me, but he'd waved his fork a little in encouragement and I'd downed it, and now we were relaxed in the kitchen; sitting at the neat breakfast bar and sipping instant coffee.

'Use your pipe, Charles, if you think it might help.'

'Thanks.'

My fingers were trembling slightly as I teased the tobacco into the bowl. I fumbled with the matches, but eventually, I was drawing okay and as ready as I'd ever be for what he might throw at me.

It started like the first tentative lines on a sketch-pad.

'This Smith – this detective chief inspector – you say he's bent?'

I nodded.

'Bent? Or over-enthusiastic?'

'He's trying to hang wife-murder round my neck.'

'He's interviewed you.'

'A very heavy interview.'

'They sometimes are, Charles. They sometimes have to be.'

'Look, I'm . . .'

'Steady, I'm your friend. I'm *still* your friend. I'm just clearing the deadwood.'

'The bastard's trying to fix me for murder.'

'And you didn't of course?'

'What?'

'Murder your wife.'

'I did *not*.'

'On the other hand . . .' He smiled. 'You wouldn't say you *had*.'

'Christ Almighty! Can't you . . .'

'Cool it, Charles.' A pause, then, 'Let's leave the murder aside for a moment.' Another pause then gently, 'You don't like cops?'

'That in spades,' I growled.

'You don't trust them?'

'No way.'

'You wouldn't want to tell them what you've told me?'

'Tiny . . .' I waved the pipe around a little. 'I *trust* you. It's that simple. Coppers? After what I've been through? You must be joking.'

'They aren't all the same.'

'I don't feel like fishing around in the box on the off-chance.'

'I know some good coppers,' he murmured. 'Some very good coppers.'

'I don't want to meet them.'

'Very good,' he repeated softly.

'I don't care,' I said harshly. 'I don't want to know.'

'That's very good advice, Charles. The best I can give you.'

'Nice going.' I know I sounded bitter. I was bitter. 'I put my neck on the block and hand you the axe and what do I get? Enough sweet-smelling crap to keep a sob sister in answers for a month. Tiny, I don't *need* advice . . .'

'Good advice.'

'. . . I need help. I know what I *should* do. I added two and two a long time ago. But if I did what I *should* do, I'd be cat's meat within days. Maybe hours. And what the cops didn't eat the other bastards would be waiting for. I thought I'd made that plain. I thought you understood . . .'

'Sure. I understand.'

'. . . but like hell you understand. Okay, I've built a wall. On their say-so, with their approval, I've built a wall.

A wall of big-band sound. 'Tiny, I'm hiding behind that wall I'm scared out of my skull, and you'd better believe that before you tear that wall down. You'd better understand something. Understand it, and don't doubt it for one minute. When you tear that wall down, friend, you'd better place an order for a wreath. It's *that* serious.'

'I know.'

'The hell you know. You wouldn't . . .'

'I know,' he repeated. He stood up from the breakfast bar and stepped across towards the stove for the coffee-pot. As he poured coffee, he continued, 'You're well up the creek, Charles, the paddle's gone and the canoe's sprung a serious leak. Now, cool it. Your pipe's out. Strike a match and get puffing.' He returned the pot to the stove, fingered two ginger snaps from a jar and tossed one in front of me. As he seated himself, he said, 'The advice was necessary. It had to be given. Okay, you won't take it – I didn't expect you to – so we move on from there.'

Some people can take over. They don't have to stamp and shout, they're just there, in their rightful place at the head of the column. Tiny was one of those people, he took over and I let him. I was glad to let him. I was glad to juggle around, smoking a pipe, feeding myself ginger snap, sipping coffee and listening. And what I heard made my hair curl.

'Right, Charles, from what you tell me you should know something about banking . . .'

'A little.'

'. . . About top league, international banking deals.'

'Not a lot,' I corrected myself. 'Mortgages and loans. After that I need a guide-dog.'

'Okay, let me tell you.' He chewed and sipped and talked, and he moved the nibbled ginger snap around to emphasise points. 'The Bank of Ireland. Lower Baggot Street, Dublin. Authorised capital, fifty million Irish Jimmy O'Goblins . . . that was the figure last time I checked, it might be a little more today. That doesn't mean it *has* that capital. It means it *can* have that capital . . . if it's lucky.

'These days it's not too lucky. Eire is going through economic hard times. Has been for years. The economy is tottering along, from crisis to crisis. Sometimes up, sometimes down, but never really able to pull itself out of its private Irish bog by its own shoe-straps. You know this. I don't have to draw graphs.

'Now, forget about guns and bombs and terrorists. They don't come into the equation. Only money. Only security. Believe me, Charles, people don't matter – national boundaries don't matter – *nothing* matters, when you shove enough noughts at the end of a figure. And enough noughts make for investment, and investment makes for economic recovery.

'But the boys who invest – the real money-bags of the world – want more than a balance sheet. Numbers in a ledger can be . . . if not actually altered at least left out. They can add up to whatever some smart operator makes them add up to. Therefore investors – big-time investors – won't look at fancy figures. Nor will they take too much notice of paper money. Remember Germany after the First World War? *They* do. They don't want *their* millions to buy only a loaf of bread. More than bread, Charles. Something more substantial than bread, therefore something more substantial than paper money. Or *if* paper money, paper money solidly backed by a commodity that never loses its value.

'Gold. That's what I'm talking about. I don't have to tell you . . . you'll have guessed it already.' He paused to give a wry smile. 'Why the hell *gold*, Charles? I've asked around. Nobody can give me a reasonable answer. Why, *specifically* gold? It's not the most precious commodity in the world. Not by a long way. Bulk for bulk, diamonds make it almost a base metal. Indeed, centuries ago, in the ancient South

110

American civilisations, it *was* treated as a base metal. By itself, it's certainly one of the most useless metals. Even when used as ornaments it has to be compounded with some stronger metal. A quirky choice. But made probably by some influential character with the stuff lying around in his back garden . . . and from that moment, everybody talked about "the gold standard"

'The phrase doesn't mean much these days. Or so we're told. But behind locked doors, it *does*. People make money by shipping gold from Point A to Point B. Fortunes! Sometimes they don't even *move* the damn stuff. It's there, sitting on its fanny, and its owner switches addresses as the price fluctuates and, as long as he has a finger on the financial pulse of the world, that's it. It keeps him in mink bed-sheets.

'Okay, we're talking about gold. Okay, we're talking about the Eire economy. Okay, we're talking about the biggest, legitimate you-scratch-my-back-I'll-scratch-yours understanding in the world. It's legit. It's done all the time. It just isn't too well *known*.

'An economy needs a kick-start towards happier days. That's Eire. It needs investors. Again, Eire. To get investors, it needs solid, financial security. Gold, in other words. And the Bank of Ireland and the Bank of England . . .'

'Bullion!' I breathed.

'Give the boy a prize. Bullion.'

'To prop up the Eire economy.'

'That's putting it too crudely, Charles. Put it this way. If the Eire economy heats up, the United Kingdom will feel the warmth. In the long term, it helps everybody.'

'So . . . bullion?'

'Shipped from Liverpool to the Emerald Isle itself.' He nodded. 'It's happened before. I've no doubt it's sometimes flown, just as it sometimes goes elsewhere, just as it sometimes comes *into* the U.K.'

111

I took a deep breath, then said, 'That makes them big.'

'They were always big.' Then very sombrely, he added, 'They were big in the small hours of the eighth of August, more than twenty years ago.' He saw my puzzled look, and added, 'Nineteen-sixty-three.'

'I'm sorry, I'm still not with you.'

'Buckinghamshire. Mentmore, near Cheddington. Between Sears Crossing and Bridgego Bridge.'

He waited, with a half-smile touching his mouth corners, until the penny dropped.

I breathed, 'Judas Christ!'

'That's how big, Charles,' he said gently.

'The Great Train Robbery?'

'Those who got away with it. Those who never appeared in court . . . with a new gang, of course.'

'That's . . .' I moistened my lips. 'Bill – Bill Wilkinson – he mentioned them once. We were chatting. Nothing in particular. But he mentioned it in passing.'

'In certain circles it's still looked on as the neatest job ever pulled.'

'It scared him. Even to talk about it, scared him.'

'It would. It scares me a little.'

'And you think it's them?'

'It's them.' He nodded with absolute certainty. He sipped coffee which was by this time almost cold, then asked, 'The Great Train Robbery. What do you know about it?'

'What I've read. In newspapers.' I said it rather hoarsely, because this little snippet of information was still rocking me. 'Not a lot, I'm afraid. Like most people, I've almost forgotten it.'

'Just to jog your memory then. The night of Wednesday-Thursday. The small hours . . . just after three and before four. The mail train, from Glasgow to London, carrying used Bank of England notes for pulping. They ambushed the train, stole a hundred and twenty sacks – made off with

112

£2,595,998 – and only small change has so far been recovered. Not more than the five thousand represented by the last six figures.

'Now, tell me, Charles – as a one-time bank official, tell me–' I had the distinct impression that he was rather enjoying himself. In the nicest possible way of course, Tiny being Tiny, but just a wee bit professorish. On the other hand, who could blame him? He knew his onions He certainly knew his train robbers. I was happy to give him elbow room. He continued, 'You have two million used, non-traceable bank notes. Two million in hard cash. How the hell do you get rid of it? More than a hundred sacks of the stuff, okay?

'It takes some hiding. There isn't a fence in the world would look at it. It's virtually *impossible* to spend. The cops and the security organisations are searching for it like crazy. You can't hand the damn stuff over some bank counter. You can't suddenly up your living-style to meet this new wealth without having flatfeet treading a well-worn path to your door. Okay, you've nicked it. But how the hell do you *spend* it?'

'Let me tell you, Charles. That raid – and it was more of a raid than a robbery – that raid was a military exercise. Right? It was a military exercise and it was for real. The driver was hurt. He was hurt pretty badly, too, but that was played down a bit . . . too many of the public were rooting for the bad guys. Maybe unwittingly, but whatever, the press made the bastards look like latter-day Robin Hoods. Just take it from me, had it been necessary, people would have been killed. With two and a half million in the kitty, life comes very cheap. But, okay, all that loot . . . what next?

'A military exercise? That means a military mind. A military mind? That means a trained soldier. A good soldier. A ruthless soldier. Certainly an officer. An officer capable of planning, and planning well. The army? Okay the army, but not *the* army, except as an original training ground. Let's say *an* army. A British soldier – a British officer who knows the ins and outs of the British banking system in general, and the Bank of England in particular – but an army which is *not* the British army. You follow the reasoning?'

'British soldiers guard the Bank of England,' I contributed.

'Indeed,' he agreed. 'Guardsmen. Every night, inside the Old Threadneedle Street Lady herself. But they're *in* the army. This guy wasn't, not any longer. He was – or recently *had* been – in somebody else's army. A mercenary. Not just some out-for-a-kick khaki job. A top-ranker, holding power in one of the so-called emergent nations. Top-ranker enough to have the ear of those who ran that nation. A little bent, perhaps. Let's be charitable and say a little desperate.

'We're back to economic prosperity again, Charles. Not *our* economic prosperity . . . the doubtful economic prosperity of an emergent nation. That and diplomatic bags. Diplomatic bags, and two million smackers without a real home. Maybe *not* diplomatic bags – that would have been a little clumsy – clumsy, but possible and possibly dangerous. Maybe a back door of a little-known national bank. Start talking at *that* level – start talking about national budgets, even the budgets of new and relatively poor nations – and two million sounds like chicken feed.'

I narrowed my eyes and said, 'You're not guessing. I have the feeling you're not . . .'

'I'm not guessing,' he admitted quietly. 'Quite a few of us aren't guessing. We worry a little because we *know*, but can't do a damn thing.'

'In that case, who the . . .'

'I've almost finished, Charles. Hold your water a little longer.' He leaned back in the chair, seemed to stifle a yawn, and ended, 'The professional way. One part of you admires it. That stolen money – the bulk of it – had a home to go to before it was stolen. Otherwise, the whole exercise was futile. And only one home was possible. That was so obvious, it was accepted within the first twenty-four hours. But accepting it and *proving* it? That's the story, Charles. You won't find it in any book, but that's what happened. A very smart raid, the biggest haul in the history of the railways, a waiting customer, then an all-mod-con villa waiting and a nice fat pension for the rest of his life. And now . . .'

'And now?'

'Either he's grown greedy or somebody else has enticed him into another venture.'

'And that,' I said suspiciously, 'makes *you* a rather special security guard. Not run-of-the-mill. You know too much. Who the hell are you, Tiny?'

I recall that conversation. I remember it very vividly; word for word. I also remember that I didn't doubt him. I realised he could have named names and could have named places, but that wasn't too important. Indeed, it was a measure of his honesty that he didn't. Had he done so it might have sounded like bragging, and anyway sometimes too intimate a knowledge of certain things can carry its own danger.

He'd told it well. He'd asked and answered *exactly* the right number of questions. Followed *exactly* the right line of logical progression.

And now he answered my question.

'I'm who I profess to be,' he smiled. 'I'm what you think I am.'

He stood up from the breakfast bar, walked out of the kitchen and returned carrying a bottle of whisky and two glasses. He opened the fridge and took out a jug of cooled water. He continued talking as he poured the drinks.

'Twenty years ago – thereabouts – I played cloak-and-dagger games. New at the job, but eager. Very eager. The train robbery took place and the police forces all over the U.K. went on top alert. The security organisations were

115

asked to help. Obviously. Coppers know crooks – crooks know coppers – somebody *nobody* knew had to be drafted in. A handful of us. We were vetted. Boy, were we vetted!' He chuckled quietly. 'They did everything short of examining our underpants.

'*That* was when I was given a false identity. Sent to an airport – one of the main provincial airports – and told to "go crook". It's not hard, Charles.' He re-capped the bottle and pushed one of the glasses towards me. 'Like flies at a jam-pot. Airports. Docks. They come sniffing around, seeking whoever's on the take. And, sadly, some of us are.'

He re-seated himself and tasted his whisky-and-water before he continued.

'For about two years we worked hand-in-glove with the coppers. Buckinghamshire Constabulary. Scotland Yard. Various Regional Crime Squads. We pooled our knowledge, retrieved a few thousand pounds . . . and eventually accepted that that was *all* we were going to retrieve. On the way, we stopped up a few local rat-holes. But we never got within touching distance of the main guy or his top lieutenants. We know who – we know how – we know where, but there's damn-all we can prove.

'Admiration? Well, I guess two heavyweights who hate each other, battling it out for the world crown . . . *that* sort of admiration. We wanted to win – my Christ, how we wanted to win! – but we lost. A fact of life, Charles. However big the crime, you can't keep on top strap forever. The case is still open, but after two years we had to ease the pressure a little. I came back to being myself and, a few years back, moved to Liverpool. But . . .' He moved a shoulder. 'We keep in touch. And over the last few months, we've heard rumours. Not the first time.' A quick, almost nervous chuckle burst out, like a bubble surfacing in a pond. 'The crafty old devil. He's sent rumours out since he settled down. Every few years. Decoys, see? Feints. Sheer professionalism. Keeping us on the hop. And in time making us think they're *all* feints. That's how good,

Charles. That's how bloody *good*.'

'You're scared.'

I made the accusation in a harsh, flat voice.

'I'm scared,' he admitted, softly. He tasted his drink, then went on, 'I know *why* I'm scared. I know the size of it.'

'A bullion robbery?'

'Uhuh . . . with trimmings. It has to be with trimmings.'

'And my job to tell them when? Having pumped details from you?'

He nodded.

'Okay, so I *don't* pump details from you. End of bullion robbery.'

'End of Charles Ryder.' He tilted his head slightly to one side and examined me much as an academic might examine a backward pupil. 'Charles, old son, you won't have to *pump* me. They won't risk me clamming up on you. That's not their style. Too airy-fairy. When you ask me, I'll be expected to *tell* you. No messing. They'll have thought up a barrel over which to stretch me. Okay, you're important, but not *too* important. Your job is to keep me from them. I know you and, as far as they're concerned, that's all I know. You're merely the conduit via which they obtain information, without actually contacting me.'

'Alison!' I breathed.

'The obvious mouth-opener,' he agreed grimly.

'What the hell can we . . .'

'She'll be taken ill. Have an accident. Anything.'

'You mean . . .'

'That's all, Charles. Not where – not when – just soon. And a private nursing home, with male nurses wearing size-ten boots.'

So the cops were in. Dammit, they *had* to be. Without actually saying so, Tiny had dropped hints as heavy as paving-stones. Very special cops – I didn't doubt that for a moment – but a cop was a cop . . . and I did *not* like cops.

For two whole days I was too worried to eat. That is no

figure of speech. I know. It happened. I was too uptight; my neck muscles, throat muscles, were too tense to allow easy swallowing; each mouthful threatened to choke me. My pipe was a permanent fixture between my teeth. I was God's gift to the *St Bruno* tobacco company. And the matches! I wasn't capable enough to light the bloody thing as it should be lit. I must have gone through three boxes of matches each day.

I tried booze. The hard stuff, and neat. It half-worked; made for a little relaxation. Then I got scared about something else. Maybe too *much* relaxation. Maybe the tongue would become too loose. So, at night, I locked myself in my room and tried solitary drinking. Throwing the stuff down, as a form of anaesthetic. As I recall one full bottle, poured at full throttle, made for slumber without getting undressed.

Forty-eight hours – thereabouts – and the combination of hunger and hangover brought a certain phlegmatic acceptance. It is, I found, impossible to stay on a high forever and still be a citizen of *this* world. Even terror can become monotonous. Even a slight bore. The point comes when, figuratively speaking, you take a deep breath and tell everybody, bar two, to go screw themselves . . . and suggest to those two that they find a quiet corner, and get busy screwing each other! Simple sanity demands it.

That was the day I slunk into Tiny's office again, and he gave me a sly and twisted smile. I understood. At some time in his life he, too, had crawled along the same dark drain.

Thereafter, we talked the weather, we talked football but, most of all, we talked jazz. The opening of hearts of the Sunday and Monday might never have happened. That's how careful we were.

When did I decide to be brave? When did I consider the possibility of medal-chasing?

The question does not admit of a pin-point answer. Like

a bad pain in the guts; something serious that you pray will go away, because you're scared of the surgeon's knife. Then the pain gets gradually worse and a decision has to be made. The deep hole or the risk of a butchering job? There is no moment when you move from 'No' to 'Yes'. It builds up, and you can't take the agony any more.

That's how it happened.

On Friday, the last day of the month, Tiny wore the required expression of worry, and said, 'Alison's had an accident.'

'Oh!'

I felt a distinct thump in my chest as my heart skipped a beat. For a moment, I thought it was for real; that the bastards had reached her.

'Nothing too serious. Nothing fatal. A broken leg. It might take some time to heal. Meanwhile, she's in a nursing home.'

'Oh!' This time it was with relief. I gave a watered-down smile, and added, 'Give her my love.'

'Yeah. She fell down the stairs at home last night. I had to send for an ambulance.'

'Painful,' I remarked.

'Painful . . . but not fatal.'

Then we changed the subject, because I wasn't going to be told any more, and I didn't want to *know* any more. And if there was a day or there was a time, that was it. Maybe I'd allowed Alison to move into the vacuum left by Judy or, if not wholly, at least in part. They were, more or less, of an age and Alison was the sort of daughter I'd once dreamed of Judy becoming. That magnificent age between the late teens and full womanhood. The mix of basic wisdom and innocence. No wiles, as yet; no smart phrases, no guile, no broken dreams. We all pass through that age, but unfortunately some of us rush ahead and don't even notice. The wise ones savour it, recognise it for what it is and don't try to push it behind them. The wise ones. The happy ones. People like Alison.

And now, Alison was safely under wraps, and that seemed to be my cue to move.

That evening, before I went up to the flat, I called in to see the old lady. It wasn't unusual. I tended to call twice, sometimes three times, each week. Why? No real reason that I can put my finger on. A habit. And whatever else she was, she was also an interesting person to talk to. It also seemed sensible. Could be I was guarding my back a little. No matter . . . I called.

We talked of unimportant things, then I slipped it in.

'Tiny's kid has had an accident.'

'Oh?'

I was watching, without *obviously* watching. I might have seen a split-second glint in the eyes. A fractional narrowing. On the other hand, I might not. These characters knew how to control themselves.

'She fell downstairs,' I volunteered. 'Broke her leg. She's in hospital.'

'Which hospital?' I think the question came out a little too quickly.

'I don't know. I didn't ask.'

The talk switched lanes and we exchanged blank words for ten minutes or so then, as I was leaving, she delivered the tag-lines.

'Do you have anything planned for this weekend, Charles?'

'Nothing specific. Why?'

'I think Sonny might come north. He may want to see you.'

'I'll be around.'

'Dinner, Sunday?'

'Thanks. Why not?' As I opened the door to leave, I added, 'There's something I'd like to tell Sonny.'

Pork chops, done to a T. Creamed potatoes. Baby brussels, fresh garden peas, diced carrots and a side salad. Thereafter bilberry pie with whipped cream, followed by freshly ground and percolated coffee, aided and abetted by liqueur brandy.

As always, the old lady put on a spread and I saw no reason not to enjoy it. Indeed, I wallowed in it. I was conscious of the possibility (I put it no higher than the possibility) that it just *might* be my last meal on earth. So, why not live high on the hog while it lasted?

I wasn't being brave. If anything, I was forcing myself to be stoical. I was quite proud of the fact that I could make it.

Then the usual armchairs, the pipe and cigarettes, the classy booze and the very civilised conversation.

'You wanted to see me about something,' he said, and his tone was its normal, friendly self.

'Me?' I played dumb. This was going to be my race and, whether I won or not, I was going to have a say in its speed.

'Ma mentioned.'

'About . . . oh!' I looked sudden remembrance. 'Oh, yes. Tiny's daughter fell down the stairs. She's in hospital.'

'Is that important?'

'Could be.'

The old lady asked, 'What makes you think that's important, Charles?'

'Okay.' I moved a hand in a palm-upward gesture. 'It's not important.'

'Important enough for you to want to tell me,' he smiled.

'I was mistaken.'

'About what?'

'Oh, forget it.' I struck a match and raised it towards the pipe bowl. 'I made a mistake.'

'No, Charles. That won't do, I'm afraid. I'd like to know why you think Tiny's daughter having an accident might be important to us.'

'Forget it.' I waved out the match.

'Please, Charles.'

'Okay.' I removed the pipe from my mouth and blew

smoke. 'You asked me to get friendly with Tiny. Tiny's kid ends up in hospital. I thought you should know.'

'As simple as that?' He made it sound like a very civilised question.

'You've made it complicated, friend.'

'Perhaps.'

She murmured, 'We have to be careful, Charles. You realise that, of course?'

'No.' I shook my head.

'You *don't* realise that?' He sounded mildly shocked.

'I don't know a damn thing.' I made myself sound a little peeved. 'How the hell can zero knowledge add up to realisation?'

'Quite.' He smiled and looked satisfied.

'We have to be *very* careful.'

'Yeah . . . you've said that already.'

He drew on the cigarette, tasted the drink then, in a very couldn't-care-less tone, said, 'Which hospital?'

'I didn't ask.'

'Maybe you should ask. To be safe.'

'You think it might be the wrong hospital?' I tried not to make it sound too dumb a question.

'What?'

'That they might not take care of her?'

'Why should *I* worry?'

'I'm wondering that myself.'

'What?'

'What's meant by "safe"? And, to use your own words, why should *you* worry?'

I realised I'd pulled a neat switch. Now, *I* was asking the questions. He tried to grab the initiative before it slipped too far.

'Ask which hospital.'

'No.'

Four words. A three-word instruction and a one-word refusal. No shouting. No tantrums. But it was like

122

slamming a door in his face. It created a piece of silence. Not long, but long enough for his eyes to harden into chisels, and that only for a moment. But I saw it, and I was meant to see it.

Then the old lady crooned, 'You're upset about something, Charles.'

'You could say that,' I agreed.

'Tell us.'

'You asked me to get friendly with Tiny.'

'Yes.'

'I did. I like the guy.'

'That's as it should be.' Sonny took over again. The same Sonny; the same quiet, buddy-buddy tone of voice. 'That makes things easier.'

'We get on fine. We like each other's company.'

'So what's the gripe?'

'You want it straight?'

He nodded.

'I don't think you'd understand.'

'Try me.'

The old lady murmured, 'I'll get the bottle,' and left her chair to walk to the booze cabinet.

I paused a moment, then started, 'It doesn't take too many brains to work out that I'm some sort of investment . . . right?'

'Could be,' he agreed, carefully.

'An investment,' I insisted. 'To put me where I am on those docks, to get me alongside Tiny, to keep me in the manner to which I've had to become accustomed . . . count it in thousands.'

He made a noise like a soft grunt.

'An investment,' I repeated.

'Go on.'

'The one thing you're *not* is an offshot of Oxfam. You don't give it away. You make an investment, you expect dividends. I'm the investment . . . Tiny has to be the dividend.'

'You're thinking too deeply, Charles.' It might have been a threat. Or a warning.

I made-believe I hadn't heard it, and continued, 'The mind of a banker, friend. A very suspicious mind. A very *mathematical* mind. Things have to add up. Tiny is worth money to you. Lots and lots of money. But not Tiny – not *Tiny* – what Tiny *knows*. And Tiny is a security guard. And you – who the hell "you" are – are as bent as a crummock. And now – surprise, surprise – Tiny's child comes into it.'

'You brought the daughter in.'

'No. All I did was *mention* the daughter. Just mention her . . . but it was enough to pull you two hundred miles north in something of a panic.'

'I was coming . . .'

'Go suck onions, friend!'

'Oh, very witty.'

Out of my eye corner I saw the old lady return to her seat. She handed the bottle to Sonny, and Sonny topped up the glasses. He was smiling, and still calm. But I knew he wasn't amused, and that the calm was the eye of a hurricane. But I'd gone too far to back-track.

I took liquid courage from the re-filled glass and continued.

'A major port. A security guard and what he knows. The child of that security guard. Certain conclusions can be reached . . .'

'Don't reach them, Charles.'

'. . . and the fact that I'm the link-man makes me a key figure. I get a certain gut feeling. That you've been paying the price of a Mini for a Rolls. That's the thing I wanted to talk about, Sonny.'

'Simple greed?' I could almost hear the grin of relief in his voice.

'We're all greedy,' I murmured.

'Sometimes, too greedy.'

'Sonny, old pal old pal, this is not an auction mart.' I stared at him, and tried to look tough. 'A security guard, a security guard's offspring, and information that security guard might have. Terrible things happen to children, these days. And if anything terrible happens to *her*, I'm left holding the filled nappy.'

'You can run.'

'If I find the space.'

'You can run,' he repeated.

'Sure.' I nodded. I made it a very tired nod, and timed the break as neatly as I was able. 'I could also run now. Tonight, Tomorrow. That takes away the risk factor. All that investment . . . all down the drain.'

'Charles, if you do anything like that, every corner you turn . . .'

'No steam-heated threats, friend. The world has a hell of a lot of corners.'

'Charles, you won't even reach the first corner.' There was a hint of sadness – or was it disappointment? – in her voice. I turned, looked first at her face, then lowered my eyes and saw the revolver. She sighed, 'I'm not a very good shot, Charles. But even I can't miss at this range.'

Be assured, it is not at all like it is shown on films or on TV. Even a master like Chandler wasn't quite right. The proverbial 'man with a gun' (in this case, woman with a gun) can be very off-putting when the gun is pointed at your own digestive system. Those muscles likely to take the first impact cringe and solidify; they work like hell to make themselves bullet-proof. Suddenly. So suddenly that it brings a gasp of shock.

Then I recognised the gun, and breathed a little more easily. I knew guns. I obviously knew them better than she did. Even at that range, I had a fifty-fifty chance.

I cocked what I hoped was a cynical eyebrow at the revolver, and said, 'With that thing, you can miss.'

She looked puzzled, but tried not to. I was saying all the wrong things.

I drawled, 'A Smith and Wesson Magnum. Model twenty-seven. Easy with that trigger, ma. The only certainty is that you'll break a wrist.'

She looked even more puzzled, and brought the other hand over to make it a double-grip.

'Now, you'll break both wrists,' I taunted. 'There's a maker's warning with that gun. "Intended for men of large build and more than ordinarily powerful physique." You're neither.' I jerked my head. 'If you *do* miss – and you will – both wrists in plaster, and a hole you can drive a bus through in that wall. All you have to do is squeeze.' I forced a chuckle. 'Y'know what? Sonny's in more danger than me.'

'Put it away, Ma.'

He believed me. Why not? I was telling no more than the truth. Maybe he knew enough about firearms. She hesitated then, reluctantly, lowered the revolver onto her lap and took both hands from the grip.

I breathed a little easier. Even experts have been known to be wrong.

Sonny leaned across, took the gun from her lap and, very carefully, placed it on the carpet alongside his chair.

I murmured, 'Now who's opened a can of worms?'

Sonny sighed then, very simply, said, 'We need you, Charles.'

'That,' I smiled, 'comes as no surprise.'

'Name your price.'

'Half a million.' It seemed a nice round figure.

'Your price . . . not the size of the national debt.'

'That's it.'

'No can.'

'Okay. Find somebody else. Let them get alongside Tiny.'

'Charles.' He sounded genuinely sad. 'If you walk out on

us, you won't live.'

'With guns like that . . .' I glanced at the Smith and Wesson.

'With *something*. Believe me . . . or check with Bill Wilkinson.'

'Bill wasn't expecting it.'

'Check on *that*, too.'

This wasn't the old lady playing at hard characters. This was the McCoy. In his own, twisted way he was even sorry . . . but that wasn't going to stop him.

I bought a few moments time, while I lighted my pipe and enjoyed a few puffs. I wasn't hurried, and I was in no personal hurry. I was up to the neck and, if I went any deeper I wouldn't be able to breathe. I killed the flame of the match by blowing smoke at it, then chose my words very carefully.

'I don't play with kids,' I said gently.

'When there's no other way.'

'I'll find another way.'

'Okay.' He shrugged. 'Leave that for a moment. And *what*?'

'Not half a million?'

'Not this side of the moon, Charles. Not even for you.'

'Okay . . . a cut of the cake.'

'Which cake?'

'Don't be ridiculously shy, Sonny. There's a cake, and it's a very rich cake. It has to be.'

'Speculation, Charles.'

'As all the experts say . . . you have to speculate in order to accumulate.'

'Okay.' He spoke very slowly. 'Let's assume there's a cake.'

'Let's assume this is Sunday.'

'I can't give you a slice.'

'What the hell's the discussion?' I smiled. 'I talk with the man who *can*.'

'I'm not kidding, Charles.'

'Nor am I.'

'He won't talk.'

'Ask him.'

'I know what he'll say.'

'First, tell him what *I* say. No slice and I blow . . . then no cake.'

'He won't stand being blackmailed.'

'That makes two of us.'

The old lady gave a deep sigh, then in a sad voice said, 'Charles, you are being *very* silly.'

'I don't think so.' I waved them silent, then continued, 'Look – both of you – the situation is not fancy. It is very simple. I do *not* play big-bad-wolf with kids. Nor do I stand around and let other people. I'm close enough to Tiny. You want something from him, that's obvious . . . I'll get it. My way, or I walk. And my way includes a piece of the kitty. At a guess without me there *is* no kitty. That's a calculated guess, and I'm making it. Okay, you have muscles. You did things to Bill Wilkinson. But if you do things to *me* . . . no kitty. That again is a calculated guess. I think you need me. If the price is right, you can *have* me. No strings, and all the way. Tell the proprietor that – who the hell the proprietor is – and emphasise that the offer is not negotiable. Take it or leave it.' Then to the old lady, 'And, Ma, don't make a habit of waving guns at people. It's not polite. More than that . . . if that thing had gone off, you might have been up to the ears in schnook.'

Robert Mitchum could not have done it better, but Robert Mitchum would only have been delivering lines. Me? I climbed the stairs to the flat with as much composure as I could collect, I locked the door, then I hurried to the bog and spewed my guts up. That's how sure I was.

I was tangling with tigers, and it was *their* jungle. And having rid myself of a perfectly good meal, I sprawled on the bed and figured myself as the biggest lemon ever to drop from a tree.

On the Thursday (May the 6th) I got part of my answer.

It was a hold-him-while-I-hit-him job, and it was performed by experts. As I locked the car door, they seemed to materialise from the brickwork. Two grabbed my arms and bounced me into a convenient alley. I opened my mouth to yell, and the third rammed home a fistful of soil. Thereafter, the going over. Brass knuckles over a leather glove, while my back was to a wall and my arms were held in a crucifixion position. Full blooded belts in the belly and damn-all I could do to dodge or ride. Then they left me and I spat my mouth clear, curled up in a foetal position and calculated my remaining life-span as being measureable in minutes.

I lived. Bent double, holding my middle and crawling along with one arm steadying myself against walls, I made it to the door, up the stairs and into the flat.

They were waiting. Sonny and the old lady. (I was too interested in other things to worry about the spare key they must have used, or the fact that they were present at the moment of truth.) I know they looked worried. Even sympathetic. Maybe they loved me after all.

The old lady said, 'There's a hot bath drawn. Get your clothes off and we'll help you downstairs.'

'You'll feel better,' promised Sonny. 'I'll have your pyjamas and dressing-gown ready for you when you've soaked.'

So they stripped me mother-naked, half-carried me down to the old-lady's place, dunked me in a steaming bath and allowed me time to recover.

I ached. God, how I ached. I'd eased myself from the bath and I'd examined that part of me which had been hammered. The heat had already drawn out the colours.

Two areas, each as big as a side-plate, and the hues ranged from deep purple to a shade of nasty liver. I'd fingered them, very gently, and I'd calculated that bones weren't broken. Everything else . . . but no bones.

And now I was in pyjamas and dressing-gown, sprawling in my usual armchair, sipping hot, sweet, brandy-laced tea and, for the first time in years, smoking a cigarette.

'We warned you,' she said, and she spoke almost tearfully.

'If . . .' I winced. I became acutely aware that stomach muscles are also part of the business of talking. I croaked, 'If I ever see any of those bastards again – anywhere, anytime – I'll kill them. Give them my compliments. Tell them to live for every hour. Because . . .'

'I don't know them' he interrupted, and his voice, too, sounded sad.

'Up a duck's arse!'

'They were paid. They did a job.'

'In that case, include the bastard who paid them.'

'Charles . . . don't,' she pleaded.

'He doesn't like being blackmailed, Charles.'

'Tell him.' I forced the words out and tried to ignore the spasms of pain in my lower half. 'Tell him – whoever "he" is – that if ever I get within reaching distance, I'll tear his balls out by the roots. Tell him that. *Promise* him that.'

She shook her head in despair, and said, 'Don't be cross, Charles.'

'Just cool it.' He forced a very watery grin. 'You're in. That's what you wanted.'

'The hell I'm in. As of now, I'm *out*.'

I didn't mean it, of course. Well, let's say that, at that moment, I meant it . . . but at that moment I was in no condition to mean anything. But as I grew accustomed to the pain, my brain started functioning and I allowed them to talk me round. I was in no hurry. Even after I'd decided to go along, I played hard to get. But not *too* hard. If what

130

I'd just gone through was the equivalent of an initiation ceremony, that was okay by me. I didn't want to pay double entrance fee.

I was into my second beaker of tea, Sonny had been upstairs and rescued my pipe and tobacco and, in a masochistic sort of way, I was even enjoying myself. They were fussing around me, even more than usual. The old lady had moved into the kitchen to warm and butter some scones. For the time being, I was king of the castle.

'And the cut?' I asked.

'Like me. Like most of us.' Sonny was back to his friendly self. 'The Colonel, and those on top, take their share. The rest is divided.'

'The obvious remark. A cut of nothing is nothing.'

'It's not like that, Charles.' He was drawing the curtain aside, inch at a time. 'We buy them, see? We *employ* people. Like we employed you. That leaves just a few of us, and the pot's bigger than you'd believe.'

'How big?'

'No.' He shook his head and smiled. 'Just big. *Very* big.'

'And this "Colonel" creep?'

'Don't ask, Charles. Don't ask . . . please.'

'That will be as much as *he* knows.'

Tiny grunted the observation, and I just caught it. We were drinking frothy coffee in a cheap, but expensive, café not far from the docks. The clientele would have made any side-show look respectable. Hair-styles ranged from punk to skin-head, from shoulder-length to Mohican. Creased trousers and jackets were at a premium and the weight of baubles, bangles and beads would have made any self-respecting Christmas tree hang its branches in embarrassment. The juke-box was going full throttle and a trumpeting elephant would have passed unnoticed. We had to lean forward, with our heads together, in order to break the sound barrier . . . but it was safe.

131

It was early evening on the next day, my midriff was still tender and I'd brought him up to date on what had happened.

'One thing,' I murmured, 'Alison's in out of the rain.'

'She stays where she is.'

'Of course.'

'That doesn't mean to say I'm not grateful.'

'Forget it.'

He tasted his coffee and ended up with a light brown moustache of froth across his upper lip. He wiped the moustache away with the back of his hand.

'I'll need to tip you off.'

'Something along those lines.'

'How?'

'Just tell me.'

'Not that easy, Charles.' He drew a thumb and finger down the corners of his mouth and he mused. 'What I am. Position of trust . . . that sort of thing. They're suspicious monkeys. Okay, I tell you. But without Alison, *why* should I tell you?'

'We're friends?'

'Not good enough. Why *should* I tell you? What reason? Why should you *ask*? Why should you be *interested*?'

'I'll think of something.'

'No. You've played it by ear long enough. You've been lucky . . .'

'You should feel my guts.'

'. . . don't let's screw things up by not being careful.'

'Okay. Come up with something.'

The juke-box changed tune. Same volume. Same badly-played guitars. Same crazy bastard on the drums. Same bawled and indecipherable lyrics. Maybe it didn't change tune. Maybe it was the same tune, played backwards.

'We get pissed,' said Tiny.

'That should be pleasant. That should help a lot.'

'Drunks talk. Share secrets.'

'Uhuh.' Light was beginning to dawn.

'We don't talk about it any more.' His eyes had that faraway look of a man working out a chess problem. 'There's a club. They have small-combo jazz every Friday night. That's where. We get stoned. Stoned enough to cause trouble. *That's how* we'll do it . . .'

Because it catered for enthusiasts, and because there aren't enough enthusiasts in the world, it was a not-too-large club. It would be rude to call it a converted cellar, but it was damn near that. In one corner of a blind alley, in one of the less popular parts of the city, it did its best with what it had. The stage was small, but the piano was an in-tune, upright Bechstein. The low ceiling helped the acoustics and the low-wattage table lights gave an air of warm intimacy.

Nor was the sound coming from the group to be sneezed at. For a semi-pro outfit they made for happy listening. All standards, but with their own variations and more than mere intro-three; they kept playing whilever anybody had anything interesting to say. *Georgia On My Mind. Riverboat Shuffle. That's A Plenty. Beal Street Blues.* They knew the oldies, without dots, and played them well.

Coming down the steps, I'd noticed the framed legend on the wall. Monday nights, Country and Western; Tuesday nights, Rock; Wednesday nights, Punk; Thursday nights, Guest Night; Friday nights, Trad Jazz . . . and so on. It had warmed my heart. Somebody had had the brains to take a whole spectrum of musical tastes, make a business out of it, and at the same time give a platform to up-and-coming talent.

It was Friday, June the 4th and that morning Tiny had said, 'Care for a spot of small-outfit jazz?'

No hint of *double entendre*. Not so much as a drooping of an eye-lid. Just the suggestion to a friend; a proposed end-of-the-week jaunt to enjoy what we both liked . . . but for the rest of the day, spiders with ice-tipped legs had worn a path up and down my spine.

And now it was closing up to 10 p.m. and the booze and the music had worked their charm and I was feeling relaxed. Relaxed, but waiting.

They were steaming their way through *Bourbon Street Parade*, and making a good job of it, when I made the remark.

'They're trying for the Jack Teagarden flip-note-two-bar bridge.'

'The Clambake Seven,' he grunted.

'Eh?'

'You're thinking about Dorsey's small outfit. The Clambake Seven.'

'I'm thinking of Teagarden, and the scratch group he gathered for record sessions.'

'You're talking out of the back of your neck.'

'Hey, Tiny . . .'

'Shut up and listen.' There was a nasty edge to his voice.

I shut up. Not because he told me, but because I wanted him to set the pace. I sensed that this was the lead-in, and I was sure when he tipped what remained of his drink down in one gulp and spilled some of it from a corner of his mouth.

At the end of the number, I murmured, 'You're juiced, friend.'

'That'll be the day.' He stood up, swayed ever so slightly, waved a hand and said, 'Drink up, stupid. My turn. Though why the hell I should drink with an arsehole who doesn't know Dorsey from Teagarden I don't know.'

'Easy, Tiny,' I said, gently.

'Drink up, you arsehole.'

I finished my drink and, at the same time, watched him. If it was acting, an Oscar was his for the taking, but I didn't think it *was* acting. The damn fool was squiffed. That hint of a slack mouth. That stupid half-grin, capable of switching to a curl-lipped snarl if the wrong thing was said.

That slight slur in the voice. No way was that *acting*.

He left the table and weaved a slightly unsteady path to the bar. Waving his arms just a little too much. Bumping into people and furniture; not hard, but enough.

A creep wearing an old-school tie and a collar shared the next table with what looked to be his wife and daughter. He leaned across, touched my arm and smiled an apologetic smile.

'Ask your friend to moderate his language, please.'

'Sure,' I grunted.

'You were right.' The smile came and went. 'It *was* Teagarden.'

'Don't tell me . . . tell him.'

'No . . . leave it.'

The big man returned. He carried two triples and banged one down on the table with force enough to jerk some of the whisky from its glass. Before he seated himself, he gulped from the other glass, then moved his head and said, 'What's *he* belly-aching about?'

'Eh?'

'That pillock.' He lowered himself carefully into his chair. 'I saw him whispering sweet F.A. to you while I was away.'

'The language, Tiny.' I frowned my anxiety. 'And take it easy with the varnish. I think . . .'

'The hell you do.'

'What?'

'Think. You haven't the sodding equipment.'

'Do you mind!' The creep at the next table joined the verbal war. 'I have two ladies with me.'

'That what they are?' Tiny squinted a slightly out-of-focus gaze, tipped more whisky down his throat, then sneered, 'You could have fooled me.'

'Tiny, for Christ's sake!'

'Of all the outrageous . . .'

'Leave it, mac.' I turned to the creep and tried an

oil-on-troubled-waters approach. 'He's drunk. I'll . . .'

'Who says I'm bloody-well drunk?'

'As a fiddler's bitch, Tiny. Don't start a . . .'

'My God! All we want is an evening's entertainment . . .'

'I'll get him out of here. Don't make things worse than . . .'

'Who'll get me out of here? You? You short-arsed sod . . .'

'Tiny! *Knock it off.*'

But it was too late. We were centre-stage, and a bouncer built like a tank was moving into action.

It was only a few yards to the door, and only a few yards from the door to the car, but a trek across the Pole was an evening stroll by comparison. The language curdled the atmosphere, tables and booze were toppled and, more than once, I laid a mental bet that the bouncer had yanked one of Tiny's arms from its socket. When the cool evening air hit him it extinguished him, and he had to be poured into the back of the Polo, and that's where he stayed until we reached his home.

Thereafter, it was pure muscle-work. The hell, he was too big to lift and carry, so I dragged. I fumbled in his pockets for the keys, and he came round enough to giggle like a schoolgirl. In the hall, I let him flop and turned to close the door.

Then I snarled, 'Now, you bloody great . . .'

'Hold it a minute, Charles.' He'd pushed himself upright, was leaning against the wall and massaging his cheeks with his palms. 'Count to twenty, slowly, then into the front room. Switch on the lights, then draw the curtains. Don't leave any cracks.'

The Lazarus act knocked me for a temporary loop, but as I followed instructions, I realised that this socking great gem might – just *might* – be more than a match for the bastards I was mixing with.

I went back into the hall, gave a shame-faced grin, and

said, 'My God, you're bloody . . .'

'You're dragging me into the front room.' He was speaking softly and gulping air. 'Time it, Charles. Time it.'

'You think we're being watched?' The thought scared me a little.

'Everything, Charles. We don't take chances on *anything*. You're dragging me into the front room. Dumping me on the couch. Taking my shoes off. Give it enough time. I'm helpless.'

We waited, and I watched him until he nodded.

'Okay. Into the kitchen. Don't draw the curtains. The cold tap. Soak a face cloth, and bring it out. On the way out, slip the Thermos jug from the working surface and bring it. It has hot, black coffee . . and I need it.'

Five minutes later, we were sipping scalding coffee, and he was telling me what I wanted to know.

'Now . . .' He looked into the lighted front room to check on the curtains. 'Upstairs. Into the main bedroom. Switch on the light, don't draw the curtains. A blanket and the eiderdown from the bed. Switch off the light, and come downstairs. I sleep on the couch tonight.'

'For real?'

'I'm stoned. I can't walk upstairs, and I'm too heavy to be carried upstairs. So you leave here and, on the off-chance that somebody *is* watching, I'd better continue the play-acting. If, after you've gone, the bedroom light is switched on, that's *us* finished. You, especially. That means I cat-nap on the couch, with the light still on, for as long as it might have taken me to sober up. Then a hot bath, a change of clothes . . . and we keep our fingers crossed.'

'He was as tight as a tic,' chuckled Sonny. 'As big as *that*, but he can't hold his drink.'

'He was drunk,' I agreed.

'Yeah. The people at the club say. Way past moderation.'

It was a hint. These creeps took nothing on trust. Tiny had been legless. I'd told them he'd been legless. So check that he *had* been legless. Tiny had been so right.

The old lady said, 'I'm glad we didn't have to involve the child.'

'It wouldn't have mattered.' Such quietly-spoken ruthlessness. Then, as if there remained some slight echo of doubt. 'We'd have been sure.'

'We're sure now,' I contributed. 'He was a drunk, boasting. Showing how much more he knew. How much more than anybody else.'

'If it's the right thing, Charles.'

'Dammit, he said he had to go in at midnight, July seventh.'

'Not a lot to go on.'

'Something special arriving at two in the morning, on the Thursday.'

'Could mean anything, Charles.'

The old lady said, 'Very unusual, Sonny.'

'Ma, we're not after the unusual. We're after a specific.'

The trick was to push it, without seeming to push it. The old lady tended to want to be convinced. Maybe she *had* a maternal instinct, after all. Why not? They pickle walnuts!

I said, 'He's never had to go in at midnight before.'

'He's never *told* you,' corrected Sonny.

'He'd have mentioned it. After, if not before.'

'I think he would, Sonny.'

'Ma, we have to be *sure*. It's a one-time operation.'

We were back at the old tea-and-scones routine. It was Sunday afternoon – the Sunday after the Friday – and Sonny had scampered north after I'd fed the griff to the old lady. And Sonny wasn't quite convinced. I think he *wanted* to be convinced. He was just a very wary bird.

I said, 'Look, Sonny, what the hell, it has to be what we're after.'

'Doesn't follow.'

'For Christ's sake!'

'Could be. It's possible. Probable. Even likely.'

'In that case . . .'

'We have to be *sure*, Charles. It could be other things. I'm not saying it is . . . it just *could* be. It's a busy dock. They export and import anything you care to name.'

'At two o'clock in the morning?'

'He said it was "arriving". That could be coming or going.'

'His office is near the gate,' I argued. 'To me, that means export.'

'To me, that means nothing. It merely *suggests* export.'

'Okay, leave it. Give me a week. I'll . . .'

'No.' He reached a difficult decision. 'Fix up a meeting.'

'What?'

'The three of us. Somewhere safe.'

'Hell's teeth! After all the work I've put in to get near him. To become his friend. And now . . .'

'Charles.' He'd made up his mind. 'If it's what we hope it is, who cares? We tighten the screw, that's all. He can hate our guts for the rest of his life. If we're sure, that's no skin off our nose.'

When you're on your own, faced with an advancing Panzer division, if you have brains, you retreat. Gracefully, perhaps, albeit reluctantly. But unless you yearn for a hero's funeral, that's the only choice you have. The decision was Tuesday – two days hence – and on Tuesday evening Tiny and I had to meet Sonny somewhere not too far away, not too crowded and not too stupid.

In Southport. Sonny's choice. 'Don't tell him what, Charles. We nail him here on our ground.' Therefore the north-east stretch of Marine Drive, by Marshside and alongside the coast, where cars are allowed to park and there is an uninterrupted view across the soiled sands of the bay and, in the far distance, twinkling lights of Blackpool form an almost fairy sky-line.

The sun was almost kissing the horizon, but without the sea it was a cheapjack production. No shimmering golden path. Just a blood-coloured sphere pulling its multi-coloured sheets around itself as it went to bed. We watched it for a few minutes – I at the wheel of the Polo, Tiny sitting alongside me, Sonny in the rear seat – and it seemed to reflect thoughts of my own life. Flash, but not brilliant. One short jump ahead of disaster. In a strange way, I'd always been the guy being told what to do. Masters at the bank; Anne at home; thereafter, Bill Wilkinson, Smith, Tommy Kelly, Sonny and the old lady. And now Tiny.

Tiny had said, 'Don't over-play it, Charles. You're not angry. You're not bitter. You're not disappointed. You're certainly not surprised . . . this is why you made friends with me.'

I'd grunted, but felt far from mollified.

'Let Sonny do all the talking. All the asking.'

'And don't think he won't.'

'I expect him to. He'll get the answers he's after . . . if he works for them.'

And now it was starting, and I stared at that big, stupid sun and hoped to hell Tiny could cream the bastards as much as they deserved to be creamed.

Sonny lighted a cigarette, moved to a position where he was talking directly between Tiny and myself, and said, 'You don't know me, Tiny.'

'No.'

'Call me Sonny. Everybody else does.'

'Do we need formal introductions?'

'To know each other,' said Sonny, gently.

'So? Now we know each other. I can't say it's made my day.'

'You got drunk Friday night, Tiny.'

'You from some cock-eyed temperance crowd?'

'Eh?'

140

'Charles said you wanted to see me. He didn't say why. He didn't say who. Just friends – and he pronounced that word "friends" – as if he wasn't too damn sure.'

'We're friends,' chuckled Sonny. 'Charles and I are friends. Aren't we Charles?'

'Yeah.'

'And Charles and you are friends . . . and you were very drunk on Friday night. Very drunk.'

'If it makes you happy. Okay, I was drunk. I made something of a fool of myself.'

'And you, a security guard.' Sonny clicked his tongue quietly.

'It's a job,' said Tiny, flatly. 'It doesn't carry an oath of fealty. I've yet to be told I couldn't take a drink.'

'To relax?'

'And because I like the taste.'

'To relax the tongue,' said Sonny, gently.

'Presumably you mean *something* . . .'

'Of course.'

'. . . but for the life of me I can't think what.'

'That extra shift you mentioned.'

Tiny scowled, but said nothing.

Sonny drew on the cigarette and, very conversationally, continued, 'The shift you mentioned when you were drunk.'

'I don't know what the hell you're talking about.'

'Wednesday, July the seventh.'

'I don't know what . . .'

'All right!' Sonny's tone hardened. 'As of now, we talk sense, big man. Charles, here. He's one of us. Always has been. Not quite the friend you took him to be . . .'

The blood-red orb had touched the horizon, and the illusion was that it was flattening out. Becoming fatter. Fat enough to burst and spill scarlet gore over all the earth.

'. . . He was put alongside, to feed us information. Last Friday, you were gassed. Charles tucked you up at home

141

and, while you were floundering around, the booze talked. A special shift, starting at midnight on Wednesday, July the seventh, until two o'clock in the morning of Thursday, July the eighth. Start from there, and fill in the empty spaces.'

Two black figures – *three* black figures – two men and a dog, moved across the darkening sand between the coast and the sun. They moved from left to right. Lonely silhouettes, trudging across sand not fit to be called sand. Dried silt from the estuary.

Tiny growled, 'You two-faced bastard, Ryder.'

From the back of my throat, I croaked, 'Forget it.'

'Tomorrow morning, I drop you. That for . . .'

'And tomorrow afternoon, *we* drop *you*,' cut in Sonny. 'You're without legs, big man. You're the mug who should have kept his mouth shut. Not Charles. You. That's *you* finished. Liverpool. Anywhere you care to go. Nothing! Security is your business, friend. The only thing you have to offer is a zipped mouth, and it can be unstitched. Think about it.'

'I'll risk it.' But it was muttered without conviction.

'Don't take too long. And at the same time think about that daughter of yours.'

'Leave Alison out of this.'

'Play ball, she doesn't even enter.'

'You're bastards, aren't you.' This time it was little more than a soft moan.

'All the way through to the marrow,' agreed Sonny gently. 'That is *our* business.' I felt a small shudder jerk Tiny's frame, then Sonny added, 'The big decision, my friend. Will you, or will you not, have grandchildren?'

The two men and the dog made their way across the soiled sands. The sun flattened out along its lower curve and the scarves of colour changed from mauve and purple towards dark grey and blue/black. Night was on its way, and Tiny was giving mumbled answers to every question

142

Sonny asked.

Then Tiny opened the door of the Polo and, bent double, weaved a way towards the low shelter of some bushes. He brought his heart up, and I watched . . . and felt great pity.

'Leave him,' drawled Sonny.

'He'll want a lift back.'

'Forget it, Charles. Forget *him*. You've done a tricky job, well.'

Sonny caught my mood on the way back to the flat. A feeling of keyed-up excitement. They were separate excitements, of course. His was the excitement of a major robbery, carefully planned and about to be executed. Mine was the excitement of having pulled the wool over the eyes of people of whom I was terrified and, in so doing, knowing that the robbery would be thwarted. Nevertheless, one excitement complemented the other, and it could be felt as we drove back to the flat.

'A fine job, Charles. A very fine job.'

I concentrated on the driving, but glanced in the mirror and saw his face and his expression. A very satisfied expression. Which was fine. *He* was satisfied. *I* was satisfied. And, sure as hell, Tiny would be feeling satisfied.

The street lighting had come on, holidaymakers were filling the pavements seeking instant happiness and, if they found what they sought, they too would be satisfied.

We dined at Simpsons in the Strand, and I'm here to tell you that this most English of restaurants is all it's cracked up to be. You pay for the best . . . you *get* the best. And what is more, you get as much as you can eat, and sometimes more than you can eat. They cater for people with taste buds and honest appetites, therefore the food is cooked in its own excellence and not, as is so often the case, goofed to hell with sauces, spices and herbs. The roast beef tastes like roast beef . . . and the chances are it was chewing grass a week before.

I enjoyed that meal. And if the truth be told, I enjoyed the company.

Four of us. Sonny and myself (we'd travelled south by train, and booked in at the Great Northern) and the two younger men. Ginger and Snowy. They were from the same carton; fighters; craftsman killers; mercenaries, and identifiable as such at a hundred yards. Their skins had that tanned creasing which only comes with months of hardship under an African sun. Their hair was cropped to near-crewcut; the one called Snowy seemed to be carrying silver hoar-frost on his skull, and his companion's hair was bleached to a corn-yellow, with glints of its original ginger speckling its healthy sheen. When they moved, and however tiny the movement, it was with smooth grace. As if their muscles had been recently oiled. They ate quietly and deliberately . . . as if, more than once in the past, they'd known real hunger.

But pleasant men and quite relaxed. Smiles rarely left the corners of their mouths and, sometimes, they reminisced quietly together, and named places – districts, villages, townships – where inhumanity had plumbed great depths. To these two, those places were mere milestones. Reference points via which they charted their lives.

A very civilised quartet that evening of Friday, July the 2nd. Two pairs who gradually became a foursome. We were, it would seem, the cutting-edge of what was to come. We were the elite – the others, whoever they were, were mere labourers, employed for a specific purpose – and we were to be finally briefed, later that night. Meanwhile we were to get to know each other. Size each other up. Become, if not friends, at least temporary companions.

The two soldiers of fortune were talking of forages and gun-battles and Snowy grinned and said, 'Remember the Yank?'

'The Yank,' smiled Ginger.

'Tell me about the Yank,' I murmured.

These two fascinated me. The expression 'innocent killers' kept flickering through my mind. It was an appropriate expression. They had killed, many times, yet they remained cheerfully innocent. Twentieth century pirates, complete with a twentieth century veneer of civilisation. Nevertheless, and at a guess, as fighting-mad as Morgan's men when the occasion demanded it. They saw no wrong in their trade. No evil. In a world which was a cauldron of a thousand different hatreds, theirs was a skill in much demand . . . but strangely *they* didn't hate.

'The Yank . . .' began Snowy. He tasted his wine and drew on his cheroot. 'American, of course. Mad as a bloody hatter. Tarzan-type. Loin cloth, bush hat and army boots. That and crossed bandoliers . . . that was him fitted out.'

'Good bloke in a tight corner,' said Ginger.

'Oh, yeah. Bloody good. He'd go down, before run.'

'Every time.'

'Anyway . . .' Snowy took up the story again. 'This river, see? About thirty yards wide. Not more than forty. We'd heard rumours of piranha. Nasty little buggers. Bad-tempered.'

'They – er – they eat people alive, don't they?' I ventured.

'Could do . . . given time.' Snowy waved the observation aside, as of no real importance. 'They nip. Bite. Make a bit of a mess. But we had to get a line across the river, see? Somebody had to swim.' He paused to enjoy a quick chuckle. 'The Yank fancied himself. Johnny Weissmuller, mark two. Stripped off, dived in and started swimming. Christ! The noise. The language.'

'Did they kill him?' I found myself almost breathless with anticipation as I asked the question.

'Christ, no.' Snowy grinned. 'Just nibbled him, all over. Looked like he'd been painted red when he hauled himself onto the other bank. Jesus, was he annoyed.'

'Tossed a couple of grenades into the water as reprisal,' added Ginger.

'A bloody carpet of dead piranhas, and all the others having a birthday party off their mates. Vicious little buggers.'

Ginger murmured, 'The Colonel pissed himself laughing.'

In as matter-of-fact a tone as I could make it, I said, 'Piranhas. They're a South American fish, aren't they?'

'Yeah.' Snowy nodded. 'Mainly.'

Like a jig-saw with a million pieces. Africa; they'd mentioned names I'd associated with Africa, and their skins had that texture peculiar to long periods in the African climate. But piranha fish; South America and a river to cross, but not with a bridge. And mention of the Colonel. And the Colonel and the long-gone Great Train Robbery.

Bits and pieces. And those bits and pieces straddled the world. *Boy's Own* adventure stuff . . . but for real. These people – the Colonel, Snowy, Ginger, Sonny, all the rest of them – they didn't just *read* about it. They enacted it. They made it come true. They were a race apart, and as such they didn't break the law. They *recognised* no law other than their own law.

And just for a moment – for one mad moment in the comfort of one of the great restaurants of the world – I envied them, and yearned to be one of them.

At a guess, it was not too far from the university buildings, nor a hundred miles from the British Museum. On the other hand, I could be very wrong. The taxi had picked us up at *Simpson's*, then dropped us in Gower Street. From there we'd clmbed into a closed van, complete with seats along the sides and with the driver's area boarded off.

Thereafter turning and twisting along streets and roads we were unable to see, but when we stopped and before being bustled across the pavement and through the ready-open door, I caught a glimpse of the stonework of the houses, Lintels and sills of grey stone; single pieces and a little too large for architectural grace. And large, small-paned windows; ugly, sash-windows. The street-lighting, too. Poor and with a yellow tinge. The place had a Victorian air and, although I didn't know the capital well enough to be certain, I guessed we weren't too far from the Cromwell Road district.

Once in the hall, the silent, middle-aged man who'd escorted us from the van, closed the door and led the way into the body of the house. He opened a door, waited until we'd entered the room, then left.

It was a large room. Well-curtained and carpeted, with a selection of easy chairs and divans, and with side-tables strategically positioned. A carriage clock on the mantle showed the time at almost fifteen minutes past midnight.

Sonny knew the place. Knew the room. He walked to a cabinet and poured drinks. He even seemed to know which booze Snowy and Ginger preferred. He didn't have to ask. He handed me what amounted to a triple-whisky, with equal parts water and waved a hand towards one of the chairs.

'Sit down, Charles. Relax.'

'Thanks.'

I lowered myself in the comfortable chair, and allowed things to happen. What else? I was in the lions' den and, although it was a very luxurious den, I'd sense enough to realise that the lions all had a full quota of teeth and claws. The trick was to live by the minute and hope whichever unfortunate guardian angel had drawn the short straw knew his job. To listen and say as little as possible. Above all else, to *agree*.

Then we were joined by the man they called the Captain. A small, slim man. About five foot seven in height – no more – with words like 'popinjay' and 'arrogance' part of any instant assessment. Short back-and-sides, with a neatly trimmed military moustache. He didn't walk. He marched. Ramrod-backed and, when he stood facing us, it was in the approved stand-at-ease position, with his hands clasped behind his back and his shoulders squared. He wore a tailor-made, lightweight safari jacket, open at the neck, lightweight army twill trousers and soft leather, khaki-coloured shoes. He looked a dandy. I had no doubts at all that he was a dandified killer.

'Sonny. Snowy. Ginger.' He stared at each in turn and bobbed his head as he spoke their names. He turned to me, eyed me coldly for a moment, then said, 'You'll be Ryder?'

'Charles Ryder,' I agreed.

'Ryder,' he repeated. 'Nicknames we accept, once they've been earned. No Christian names.'

'Ryder,' I agreed, gently.

'You're on trust, Ryder,' he snapped. 'Word from the Colonel.'

'Thank you.'

'Don't waste time thanking anybody.' A frosty smile moved his thin lips. 'Just obey orders . . . to the letter. No one-man-band antics, otherwise you'll have damn-all to thank *anybody* for. Is that clearly understood?'

I nodded.

'Right. The others know the pattern. This is a briefing. The only briefing you'll ever get, so concentrate. Remember every detail. Excuses – explanations – they're not accepted. You'll be *where* you're supposed to be, *when* you're supposed to be, and you'll do *exactly* what you've been told to do. You'll listen. When I've finished, if you have any questions, you'll ask them. Questions. Not opinions. Not suggestions. When it's all soaked in, you'll leave here. You'll meet me, Snowy and Ginger at the scene of the operation. Until then, you'll keep your mouth tightly closed. You will *not* get drunk. You will *not* fornicate.' He paused then very pointedly added, 'Any leak, it will be from you. We won't even waste time asking. That's it, Ryder. All clear? All understood?'

'Understood,' I murmured.

'Right.' He seemed to unbend ever so slightly. He began talking slowly and for the first few sentences remained rigidly at the at-ease position, but after that he moved, stiff-legged, hands clasped behind his back. Three paces, about turn, three paces, about turn. Sometimes he threw his head back and stared at an angle up at the ceiling. Sometimes he dropped his chin and stared at the carpet in front of his feet. But although the sentences were short and crisp, there was never the hint of hesitation. Everything was now known. Everything had been worked out. And, although what he said sounded like something from a badly-made film, it *wasn't*. It was real. To these people, it was as near normal as to make no matter . . . but to me it was quite terrifying.

'Thursday, July the eighth. The early hours of the morning. Between one o'clock and one-fifteen. Bullion, delivered at Liverpool for shipment to Dublin. It comes from the vault of the Bank of England. It travels north along the M1, to junction twenty-five. Then it leaves the motorway network, crosses the country via the A52, through Derby, onto the A523, Macclesfield, A537 and onto the west-coast motorway, and from there to Liverpool. Liverpool, between one o'clock and one-fifteen in the morning. Aboard in time for the first tide.

'Transport, an armoured van, disguised in Telecom livery. Unmarked police cars as escort. One ahead. One behind. Plain clothes officers. The assumption is that they'll be armed. Handguns . . . but don't discount pump-operated shotguns.'

He paused. Not for effect, but to collect his thoughts.

'The target is approximately ten million. The ingots will be in boxes. We load the boxes into our own vans, then-drive to a destination. Helicopter. Then ship. We – we five

149

– accompany the gold. Before we see land again, it will have been melted down. Impossible to identify. Ready for sale. Ready to *be* sold . . . with the buyer ready to purchase at an already agreed price.

'Dress for the operation. Dark track-suits. Wool skull-caps. Rope-soled sandals. Black leather gloves. Camouflage paint on the faces. Each man to be geared up before he arrives at the rendezvous.

'Snowy. Ginger. On the morning of the seventh, you'll each be told where to collect a van. In the back, tarpaulin. Under the tarpaulin, the weapons. Uzi SMGs, each with two spare magazines. Two SMGs in each van. Snowy, you hand the spare Uzi to Sonny when you arrive at the rendezvous. Ginger, you do the same to Ryder.

'The first task. To stop the armoured vehicle and, at the same time, immobilise the police cars . . .'

'They'll kill you, of course.'

I grunted. It was meant to be a noise meaning I didn't care too much. But I *did* care. I cared a hell of a lot and, because I wasn't a complete mug, I'd reached that conclusion before the end of the briefing and had lived with it ever since. Nor had it been a happy thought with which to seek sleep each night.

'They took a calculated risk.' At a guess the drawl was Eton-born. Eton . . . but with solid gold plating. It had that quiet, unflappable quality which comes only with the firm knowledge of where the next meal, and the meal after that, is coming from. 'They took you for a greedy man. Not the bank robbery, of course. But the money you accepted from Wilkinson. Not *quite* honest. They needed you next to Tiny. Butter you up a little. Promise you a happy-ever-after ending. Even let you in on the briefing. Then when you've served your purpose, eliminate you. One among many.'

He chuckled, quietly.

He thought it was funny. I didn't.

150

I muttered, 'Leave nobody alive. That's what the bastard said.'

'Quite. Dead men telling no tales . . . that sort of thing. It goes with the profession.'

God! When I'd tried to pass the information on to Tiny. That hate-filled snarl. 'Get lost, you low-life, two-timing sod.' I'd believed him, and for days I'd been in a muck-sweat. Lonely. As lonely, as lost, as defeated as a man stranded on a polar ice-cap. And as frightened.

Then (this morning) the skipper of this rusty old tub had questioned the Bills of Lading.

'The quantity's wrong. Have a word with the mate. He's up on the bridge.'

Thereafter, the drawling man with the Eton accent.

'Not a very admirable profession,' he added.

'A little mind-boggling.' I stared across the tops of the warehouses as I spoke. Gazed at the twin Liver Birds perched on top of their respective towers. Liverpool's landmark, and maybe better known – maybe even more important – than the duo of cathedrals. 'Ten other men, employed on a strictly need-to-know basis. Like so many expendable beasts.'

'They work it that way. They did on the train job.'

'Same crowd?'

'Same nucleus.'

'They didn't kill that time.'

'A weakness they've strengthened.' I waited. The stench of the city drifted over the docks and twitched my nostrils. Basic poverty and decay, spiced with those masculine scents of every quayside. Tar. Paint. Oil. All fused with the smell of the sea; the tang which, to some men, is a vital part of their lives. He continued, 'This one's bigger than the train robbery. Much bigger. Bigger, therefore more final. The – er – "employees", when they robbed the train, learned things. Put two against two and came up with a big fat four. Then when they were inside, they talked and *we*

151

learned things. What little we know we learned from the hewers of wood and the drawers of water.' He paused, then said, 'A mistake they don't intend making this time.'

'Closing everybody's mouth,' I said flatly.

'And, of course, increasing the personal take. A certain logic.'

'Terrifying logic.'

'*Their* logic. The only logic they understand.'

I shuffled the Bills of Lading and, for effect, we bent our heads over them in a pantomime of examination. I flicked a glance sideways at him before I spoke.

'You're not the mate of this old tub.'

'As far as you're concerned.'

'Look,' I pleaded, 'I want something specific to hang onto. Some hint of hope that I'm not tackling a whole jungle of tigers armed only with blind faith.'

'They won't be allowed to kill you,' he drawled confidently.

'They plan to,' I grunted. 'We both agree on that.'

'They plan to steal the bullion . . . but they won't.'

'If that's the best you can . . .'

'Look!' He stabbed the Bills of Lading with a grimy finger. His expression registered anger, but not his tone. His tone carried quiet, soothing confidence. 'You're being tailed. So is Tiny . . .'

'Jesus Christ!'

'. . . But don't look for them. *They* have friends, too. Don't worry, Ryder. You're an amateur, but you're surrounded by professionals.'

It isn't easy. To know you're being tailed, and to pretend *not* to know. It isn't easy not to glance at reflections in shop windows. To pause at street corners and cast a quick eye at all the other pedestrians. Or the parked or crawling motor cars. It was a little like being part of a peep-show, but being unable to identify the knot-hole through which the stranger's eye gazed.

I found myself putting on something of an act. Not deliberately. The last thing I wanted was to give the game away. Nevertheless, it was impossible to behave normally. *Really* normally. Dammit, I almost wanted to *impress*. I was conscious of an audience, albeit an unseen audience, therefore the urge was there to give them a show. My driving was faultless; always the seat-belt, always the correct speed, always the right lane, always the perfect signals. In the rush of traffic, when the docks closed, I was a bloody nuisance. My manners, as I jostled along pavements thick with seasonal holiday-makers were impeccable. I found myself quietly apologising every twenty yards or so. Retrieving beach balls which had wandered onto the roadway. Toeing empty mineral cans nearer to the kerb-edge. In the crowded boozers, making no comment when some oafish-type elbowed his way past waiting customers and jumped the queue at the bar.

To impress, but at the same time to become invisible. I didn't want anybody to *notice* me. The complete norm. The absolute average. To be ignored. To do nothing – nothing at all – likely to encourage comment.

When I could gather my thoughts together enough to use them properly I pondered upon the slim guy with the Eton drawl. The so-called 'mate'. Eton was not the forcing ground for coppers, any more than it was the start-line for mates of rusty coasters. So . . . what? Starting with the not-too-difficult conclusion that this whole set-up was part of a league way above normal cops-and-robbers games, that thinned out the possibilities. Not robbers. Mercenaries. Soldiers, but very special soldiers. Very hard-nosed and ruthless soldiers. So . . . face them *with* soldiers. Equally hard-nosed. Equally ruthless. Something even more special than *they* were.

It *had* to be S.A.S.

Oh, sure, I was guessing. And maybe the guessing was

based, at least in part, on wishful thinking. But it seemed possible – even probable – and the public school guys came from a template the Army liked and, of the best, the S.A.S. was a choice they were given.

The thought – the possibility – buoyed me a little. Elbowed the trembles aside at night. I'd lay there and wonder. Was he outside? This guy – maybe even these *guys* – detailed to keep a watching brief on my miserable body. Out there in the summer night? Standing in some shadow and bored to hell? Watching the flat, noting the time I switch off the light? A bodyguard of sorts, maybe? Orders to dive in and pull a rescue job if necessary?

Boy's Own stuff, nothing less. A latter-day George Smiley out there in the darkness. Or maybe James Bond or Harry Palmer.

The hell!

Up there in the concave of my skull, I was brewing day-dreams. I was no agent. No counter-agent. Me? I was some insignificant fly caught in a web I'd never even known the existence of. Christ Almighty, I was Charles Ryder, a once-upon-a-time bank clerk, who'd stumbled his way into a gold-plated sewer, and couldn't find his way home. Some crazy twist had landed me up to the ears in bullion bars, and Uzi sub-machine-guns, and God only knew what else.

And I was *dead*. Already *dead*!

I was mooching around on borrowed time, breathing loaned air . . . and there wasn't one damn thing I could do about it.

Run? Did I hear somebody mention the possibility of making a run for it? Do not think I had not toyed with that idea. To run. To hit the tall timber. To be 'missing'. Since the realisation of how big a mouthful I had bitten off had dawned. Since then that possibility had been kept in mental reserve, should the heat in the kitchen become unbearable. There in the background. The final opting out.

But no more . . .

Since my conversation with the Etonian guyed up as a mate of a tramp steamer, that door had been closed, locked and bolted. The ungodly were keeping tabs on me. So were the *godly* . . . tabs on me, and tabs on the *un*godly. I was, it seemed, surrounded by a wall of invisible watchers. Who the hell was I going to dodge? I was the Joker in both packs, and no way was I going to be allowed to slide away up some sleeve. I was there to be played. Indeed, without me there'd be no game.

It seemed I had lived for this ridiculous moment. For this outrageous o'clock, to be dressed in this dark track-suit and rope-soled sandals. My face had been formed to take the black goo of streaks of camouflage paint, and my skull to be covered by the clinging woollen cap. This was, it would seem, the climax and the reason for it all.

A false state of mind, of course. The back-lash of prolonged worry and the product of living on raw nerves for days on end. And yet, strangely, a not uncomfortable feeling. It carried a certain and unusual tranquility. Worry was a thing of the past, if only because it was far too late to worry. The next few hours would end it . . . one way or the other.

Sonny whispered, 'You okay, Charles?'

'Fine.'

We were spaced on both sides of the road, along the middle leg of a Z-bend. Tucked behind grass banks, topped by hawthorne hedges. We'd approached across the fields, and we'd been there more than an hour. At a guess we'd be there at least another hour.

'Won't be long now.'

I grunted.

Sonny *was* worried. His voice, although whispered, was an odd semitone higher than normal. Periodically, I could hear his fidgeting around in the grass. As if he couldn't settle. As if the thought of what was to come refused him quiet.

Across from us, and still along the middle leg of the Z-bend, Snowy and Ginger were silent and motionless. I knew they were there, because they'd crossed the road to take up positions. They were trained men and, moreover, well-trained men. Invisible and unheard. Not a sound and not so much as a movement of grass.

The normal late-night A523 traffic passed along the road. The headlamps made tunnels of light, bordered by the hedges, but we were unnoticed. Ahead of me, and slightly to my right, I could see a slight glow in the sky, and I took it to be the reflection from Macclesfield. We weren't far from the Cheshire boundary, with Staffordshire only a little way over our shoulders. The place, the time, when the bullion carriers might be expected to be least alert; the reach towards the small hours, and more than half the journey completed; the sub-conscious feeling that, should a hold-up be contemplated, the obvious places would be at the start or at the end of the journey, therefore the mid-section being the least dangerous stretch of the ride. These men – this 'Colonel' – considered everything. To out-smart them would not be easy.

For want of something better to do, I contemplated the future.

It came as a slight shock to remember that I was still a suspected murderer on the run. That Smith and his colleagues were still anxious to put me inside. That whatever the outcome of this night's activities, my troubles were far from over.

Who the hell had killed Anne? And why?

Assuming the crowd I was supposedly a part of *didn't* finish me off – assuming Tiny and the people *he* represented out-foxed these superbly trained killers – what then? A murderer was walking the streets and, until he was traced and convicted, I could never claim my true identity with

156

any degree of safety. A beard and a broken nose added up to meagre shelter . . . but that's all I had.

Some bastard had robbed me of genuine liberty. Some bastard – some unknown bastard – had been directly responsible for all the hardship and hole-in-the-corner existence of the past months. Dammit, I *owed*. I owed, and I'd collect. At the moment, I had worries enough for ten men, but let me get out of this and I'd find him. I yearned for what I'd once taken for granted. A true identity. A name of which I was not ashamed.

Just let me ride this particular tiger . . .

I occupied my mind by going over the details of the plan, as itemised at the briefing. The van would be identified half a mile before it reached the ambush. To the south and beyond the bend, a secondary road junctioned into the A523. An empty bowser was waiting, and the driver's job was to allow the first police car and the van to pass, then crash the second police car and, at the same time, block the carriageway.

It was a tight Z-bend, therefore with any luck, the van would be out of rear-mirror sight of the accident, and into the straight stretch of the Z.

To the north, another secondary road hit the main road, immediately after the bend, and another truck was waiting to knock out the leading police car if possible, but in any case to block the road north of the Z-bend. The bullion van would be trapped and at that moment 'the Captain' would let fly with an 84-mm Carl Gustav Infantry anti-tank weapon, loaded with a low-charge projectile. *That* would certainly demolish the van; open it up ready for the removal of the bullion.

Men with fire extinguishers were ready to deal with any petrol blaze.

Thereafter, the transfer of the boxed gold bars to our own trucks, waiting in the two side-roads and, after that, the Uzi SMGs.

'Nobody to be left alive, gentlemen. Each Uzi will be fitted with a 40-round box magazine, and each of you will have a spare mag. We are employing ten men. One on the tanker, one on the truck, the other eight to handle any possible fire and to assist with the movement of the boxes. Add to that two men in the armoured vehicle and three – no more than four – in each police vehicle. No more than twenty, all told. They're not idiots. We can't afford to employ idiots. As with the police. As with the armoured vehicle personnel. However careful we are they'll see things, hear things. Self-preservation demands they must not be allowed to *tell* things.'

So easy. All you need is a vacant lot where the conscience should be.

No doubt about the Uzis. They'd perform well. Developed by a master gunsmith – a Major Uziel Gal of the Israeli Army – they were a logical step forward from the Czechoslovac VZ-23 and already adopted by German and Dutch armies. And other, less reputable, armies. If what can be easily carried and kills at a fantastic rate can ever be called 'good', the Uzi hadn't an equal. They'd die. Every last one of them. That was the function of the Uzi SMG. That was the sole reason for its existence.

Me?

Sure, I too had an Uzi, *and* a spare magazine. And I'd better be ready to use it. That or stop a burst of 9mm bullets.

It wasn't a pleasant thought. Nor, come to that, was it a nice choice, but at a guess it was a choice I'd soon have to make.

I puzzled my way through some very fundamental questions. For example . . . who'd been quietly detailed to stop *me* from talking? I was a 'must'. Other than the select band who'd been in on this thing from the beginning, I knew more than anybody. Of them all, I *mustn't* be allowed to live. I already knew far too much.

Sonny would do it . . . of course. Sonny, because we knew each other. I knew him better than I knew the other three and, because of that, I trusted him. In a manner of speaking, we were buddies. He it had been who'd first enticed me into this intrigue. Who'd gently talked me into becoming part of their eyes and ears. Who'd broken bread with me, and boozed with me, and been my slightly special friend. For sure, Sonny was detailed as Judas.

And all this – all this planning, all the coming pain and bloodshed – all this . . . merely for money. The little banker left in me revolted at the thought. Money! Wealth! Gold!

Would it buy a Christmas like my last Christmas in the Dales? Could it purchase that priceless tranquility I'd known with Tommy Kelly? Might it pay for the resurrection of Anne and, if it did, could it buy the joy of those first few years of our marriage?

That was the measure of money. The true limitation of wealth. It could do damn all. All the gold we planned to lift, plus all the gold left in the Bank of England vaults, plus all the gold in Fort Knox . . . put it all together and it couldn't buy an extra second of any day.

The only bloody thing money could buy was misery. Show me a millionaire and I'd show you a jerk who, despite the surrounding finery, was deep-down miserable. Whose happiness was as shiny and false as a plastic tulip. I'd met them. I'd rubbed shoulders with them. They had everything, therefore they didn't know what the hell they *wanted*. Just something. Something they couldn't put a name to. They'd no ambition, because they had no need for ambition, which meant they had nothing to aim for. Therefore, rudderless. Going nowhere. Nothing to divert their attention from that last hole in the ground. They were the world's . . .

A pencil-torch to our left gave two quick winks of light.

Sonny breathed, 'They're here! Second one round the corner.'

The shooting started before the second set of headlights rounded the bend. The distant crackle of small-arms fire, but not the sound of one vehicle crashing into another. The bowser had been taken care of.

The headlights stopped, doors banged open, then the rattle of a half-track being driven at speed from the left. I waited, half-ducked, for the blast of the Carl Gustav, but it never came. Instead, stun grenades.

They lived up to their name. Blinding flashes, combined with mind-shattering noise. They brought momentary blindness and a numbness of the brain; a cloying curtain of sound and light from behind which the fire-fight could be heard building up to a crescendo. Figures in battle fatigues moved swiftly and purposefully through the flash and smoke. A couple of parachute flares lighted the scene as if it was noon, and I retained enough wit to turn and seek the figure of Sonny.

He was there, panic and fury etched on his black-streaked face. Squirting short bursts from his Uzi at any S.A.S. man he chanced to spot. Up on his feet, screaming empty defiance . . . but not even looking in my direction.

They tumbled out of the half-track, and one of them was a big man, carrying a Stirling SMG at the hip. I recognised the build, I recognised the shambling run, and I saw Sonny turn at the shoulders to bring the Uzi in line.

I screamed, '*Tiny!*' but knew it was too late. He'd stop, search for me in the small hell brewing up around us, and give Sonny time. But it was too late. I'd yelled and Tiny paused, and as Sonny squeezed the trigger, the front of Tiny's blouse seemed to unstitch, and his guts spilled out before his knees buckled . . . and he was still looking round for me with a stupid, puzzled expression on his face as he died.

It was time my own Uzi spoke. Long past time.

I was on my feet. God only knows when I'd scrabbled

upright, but upright I was, with knees slightly bent and turned towards Sonny, and the Uzi was in line with his middle, at a range of less than six yards.

I croaked, 'Die, you bastard,' held the SMG rock-steady against the front of my ribs and squeezed.

I saw Tiny die. I saw Sonny turn and grin. I heard more stun grenades and saw the eye-scorching glare of the flares. Then the pain hit me, and I felt warm liquid saturating my right side, looked down and couldn't see either the hand, the arm or the Uzi.

As I passed out a final brilliance pierced my mind. A final realisation. They'd spiked the bloody gun. They'd plugged the barrel of the Uzi. I hadn't been holding a sub-machine gun. I'd been holding a blasted bomb, and when I'd squeezed the trigger I'd exploded that bomb and blown a bloody great hole in myself.

A final realisation.

A wonderful way in which to wish the world 'Goodnight'.

I spoke to God. I was good and mad with Him, too. There He was, surrounded by this mystical haze, smiling down at me through His neatly trimmed beard, as if He'd done something very special. Very bloody sure of himself . . . and I was damned if I could see why.

I said, 'You let Tiny die, you louse. You could have done something. He has a kid, waiting for him. Why the hell didn't you think of *her*?'

That's what I said, and I meant it. But the words didn't come. Just the thought. But that was okay. He could read thoughts, too.

He smiled through the muslin veil which separated us, and spoke. Plummy words which seemed to have to push their way through cotton-wool. He didn't answer my question. Not God! Far too big an opinion of His bloody self. Odd . . . He had a Geordie accent.

So, I railed at Him. Everything I knew. All the four-letter filth I could drag from the scrapings of my mind. And this time I *talked*. Mumbled. Let Him know what. Told Him what a ring-tailed, solid gold sod He *really* was.

It seemed to amuse him, so what the hell?

I decided to ignore the creep.

It was Sunday, July the 11th. I know the date, because I heard voices. Female voices. They were outside my line of vision, but I heard one of them ask what day it was, and I heard the other answer.

I blinked a couple of times, and focus came back to my eyes. I moved my head a little, and saw the owners of the voices. No, they weren't angels. Well, maybe they *were*, but if so they wore nurses uniforms, and one was busy making notes on a form fastened to a clip-board, while the other was earthly enough to be hoisting her skirt backside-high in order to check that her tights weren't crooked.

I tried to raise a hand, couldn't, but managed a croaked, 'Hi.'

The nurse with her tights on the twist hurriedly dropped her skirt, blushed, for a moment looked angry then put on a shamefaced grin.

The one with the clip-board stepped to the bed, and said, 'Nice to have you back with us, Mr Ryder.'

'I've been dead,' I whispered, solemnly.

'Pretty near.'

'All the way to Heaven,' I insisted.

She gave a quick chuckle, then said, 'The language you used to the surgeon when he came to check that the dope was wearing off. That wasn't Heavenly talk.'

'Oh!'

'Thirsty?' The other nurse moved nearer and brushed her skirt into final position as she asked the question.

'Hungry.'

'Just a drink.'

The one with the clip-board added, 'Gently does it, Mr Ryder. You're a very lucky man.'

Lucky! I was a combined plumber's nightmare and an electrician's dream. I was the link-man to a bank of machinery and the no-return terminus to about a dozen tubes. To say nothing of the bandages.

Later, when I was out of that tiny intensive care unit and in a more-or-less normal side-ward, I learned that I had been on the table a full five hours. That a surgical team had performed miracles of on-the-spot improvisation in order to sew the mangled bits and pieces back together again. That, having performed this miracle, the surgeon had stripped, washed, sighed then said, 'That's all I can do. Anything else is up to the Almighty.'

Well, the Almighty hadn't been listening when I'd cursed him up hill and down dale. He'd obviously added *His* required weight.

Not that it was a hurried recovery. What progress I made I had to take on trust when it came to a day-to-day basis. *My* only measurement was by the week. Each Sunday I'd cast my mind back to the previous Sunday and, by stretching the imagination, I saw and felt improvement.

I was going to live, and that was nice. Tiny was dead, and that was nasty. I'd be able to walk, given patience, and that was nice. I'd be without a right arm, and that was nasty. Nice and nasty . . . see? The news was fed to me in crumbs. Like crumbling a piece of shortcake and allowing me a taste. Sometimes it tasted good. Sometimes it damn near choked me.

On the 19th I was moved into a neat little side-ward, and the next day (Tuesday the 20th) I had my first visitor. The Eton-voiced man who'd guyed himself up as a ship's mate.

He brought me a bundle of paperbacks – Chandler, MacLean, Innes, Le Carré – then settled down in a cane armchair for what was obviously going to be a fairly prolonged stay.

'You've been winged rather badly,' he drawled.

'One way of putting it.'

'Our fault.' He fished pipe and tobacco from the side pocket of his lightweight jacket. 'We had the Sonny character in our sights every second.'

'Why the hell not down him before he slaughtered Tiny?' I growled.

'Another mistake, I'm afraid.'

'Oh, for Christ's sake!'

'Ryder, old man, it was a *battle*. Casualties . . . and all that. Part of the price.'

'Too high a price. There's a daughter.'

'She's with her aunt. She's being taken care of.'

'She's a bloody orphan. She shouldn't be.'

'Quite,' he agreed calmly.

There was a 'No Smoking' notice fixed to one wall of the room. Maybe they didn't teach them to read at Eton. On the other hand, maybe he figured the notice only applied to lesser mortals. Whatever, he fingered ready-rubbed flake into the bowl of a bent Peterson and lighted the tobacco with a fancy gas-lighter.

'The bullion was saved?' I asked.

'The bullion was never in danger, old boy.' He exhaled tobacco smoke from pursed lips. 'Once we knew, we switched dates. Switched transit arrangements.'

'Therefore, all for sod-all?'

'Not at all. We've well-salted their tails.'

'You sound remarkably satisfied,' I sneered.

'Surely. Why not?'

'Tiny . . .' I began.

'He volunteered, old boy. Insisted. He knew the risk.'

'He was my friend.'

'I knew him, too. Rather liked him.'

'I don't have too many friends.'

'You'll be quite a hero.'

'Damn being a hero!' I exploded. 'This whole bloody shambles needn't have happened. All you had to do was . . .'

'Ryder, it was too good to be missed. It was *necessary*.'

'They'll do it again. Something else. Something even bigger.'

'No.' He shook his head. He was quite certain.

'You got this "Colonel" bastard?'

'No. He never puts himself in a position . . .'

'So? All we've done is squat on a flash pot and farted.'

'Rather more than that, old boy.'

'I'm damned if *I* can see what . . .'

'My dear chap, we've removed his organisation. He's like Wellington without troops.'

'You hope.'

'We *know*.' He paused, puffed the pipe meditatively for a few moments, then drawled, 'Guards on the door, of course. Then a bodyguard until something more permanent can be arranged.'

'Eh?'

'You've screwed things up for the old boy.' He grinned a lazy, almost tired grin. 'Word has it he's already put a price on your head.'

'Who?'

' "The Colonel".'

'Bloody marvellous!'

'Men with long guns will be trying to collect.'

'And is that supposed to cheer me up?'

'It's why I'm here, Ryder. To put you in the picture.'

'Let's talk about Alison,' I growled.

'Alison?'

'Tiny's kid. Dammit, you don't even know her name. That's how bloody interested you are in . . .'

'She's in no danger. She's with an aunt.'

'Those two statements don't form a logical progression.'

165

'Ryder, old fellow, why should anybody be interested in Tiny's daughter? What has *she* done? She seems a sensible child. She'll cry a little, but she'll get over it . . .'

'You cold-hearted . . .'

'. . . She obviously loves her aunt and uncle, and they love her. We'll keep a weather eye on her, of course, but *you're* our main concern.'

'I'm something of a nuisance . . . is that it?'

'One could put it that way. A slight inconvenience.'

'So, why didn't you put a few rounds in me?' I asked, coldly. 'Why let me live? Why not leave me to bleed to death? When you and your soldier boys were shooting off your guns, why not point one in my direction? End of "inconvenience". Nobody the wiser.'

'We toyed with the idea.'

'Christ!'

'Then – because we tend towards magnanimity – we decided you deserved rather more than that.'

There are certain conversation-stoppers, and this was one of them. All the aggro. All the sweat and suffering. And for what? To have my own side contemplate giving me the swift chop as a means of removing an 'inconvenience'.

So – question: who were the 'goodies' and who were the 'baddies? And where the hell did that leave *me*?

'Look at it from our point of view.' He might have been quietly explaining a not-too-complicated chess move. 'You're a bank wallah. You're untrained. A trained soldier we can deal with. We understand him. He's been drilled to react in a given way. Put him in a battle condition, and he'll fight. He'll obey orders. If he's wounded, he'll accept it as part of his job.

'But you? You've been living on your nerves for months. You've been alone. One man against an organisation. Then when things happen, instead of coming out unscathed – or even being killed – you end up with the very devil of a disability. One arm amputated. Your side blasted to hell.

God only knows what else. You'll feel sorry for yourself . . .'

'With some cause.'

'Indeed, old boy. With some cause. But that's the unknown quantity. That's what's scaring us a little. What will you do? How will you react?'

Very tightly, I said, 'I haven't yet decided, but if *you* stay here much longer it's likely to be the very beaut of a decision.'

'See?' The slow grin came and went. 'It's there already. A frightening lack of objectivity.' He quietened me with a wave of the pipe. 'The facts, old man. I'll give you them . . . then think about them. There's a reward. A big reward. The insurance people lash out rather grandly in these cases. All yours. Live moderately, and you'll have no more money problems.

'There's an armed guard out in the corridor. There'll be one round the clock. And when you leave. Then – a few months from now – a completely new personality. A new name. A new identity. Overseas, if possible. Canada, perhaps. Australia. New Zealand. We can discuss the details later. Then – a couple of years from now – just token contact, to see things are moving along slowly.'

'Australia?'

'If that's where you fancy.' He nodded.

'Canada? New Zealand?'

'The choice is yours, old boy.'

'Is it?' I said, flatly.

'The media people don't even know you exist. No problem there. You won't be hounded.' The drawl didn't change. He was so damn sure of himself. He chuckled quietly. 'Pitched battles in rural England. That's definitely not *on* . . . not even for a multi-million-pound bullion robbery. Therefore, D-notices all round.'

'There wasn't a robbery.'

'Must let the chap on the Clapham omnibus sleep soundly at night.'

'The damn bullion wasn't there to steal.'

'All this cowboy-and-indian stuff. Definitely not *on* . . . officially, of course.'

'I was there,' I said, harshly. 'Remember? The idiot you let live. The lunatic who is now something of an "inconvenience". I know exactly when and where the shooting started. Some considerable time before your people reached the spot where our guns were.'

'*Your* guns?'

'You know what I mean.'

'A slip of the tongue. The sort of slip we're afraid of.' It was a friendly enough smile, as he eased himself more comfortably in the armchair. 'The wrong pronoun, old boy. And if the wrong person heard it . . .'

'It came out.'

'Of course. *You* know that. *I* know that.' The lazy grin again. 'The chappie on the door. The guard. To keep people out? Or to keep you *in*? Could be either.'

'I killed nobody,' I breathed.

'What the bull-fighting gentry call the Moment of Truth. Officially, you weren't one of us. Sadly, the only witness capable of saying you *were* isn't with us any more. Sonny. The old biddie from Southport. Ginger. They've all named you . . . as one of *them*.' The pause was perfectly timed. Then, 'You haven't many trump cards left . . . wouldn't you agree?'

When he'd gone – when he'd calmly and quietly blocked all the bolt-holes – I felt sorry for myself. No longer angry. No longer disgusted. Just sorry, and not a little afraid.

That old eight-ball was still there, and I was still tucked in close behind it. The world was peopled by smooth-tongued scoundrels, and they were all eyeing *me* with eager anticipation.

Therefore, it wasn't a real decision. I had no option. I was still linked to drips. I carried more bandage than the

168

average Egyptian mummy. So, what the hell but to let the damn thing ride along at its own pace? What else was possible? Part of me was missing; but I was still alive . . . and that was more than I'd once expected.

That having been said, there is nothing easy about learning to live with only three limbs. Maybe that saved me. The concentration needed to perform even the simplest of tasks. I was born right-handed. For more than two score years I'd been a right-handed animal. Now I had to re-learn everything, and become a *left*-handed animal. Writing. Combing my hair and beard. Even reading . . . to learn to turn the page with the left hand.

I got mad with myself. That first day when I was allowed to leave my bed. The business of draping a dressing-gown across my shoulders. I swore at that dressing-gown, as if it was *its* fault. I was one-armed and one-handed. More than that, I was *wrong*-handed. The futility and stupidity of cursing the dressing-gown struck and, instead, I cursed myself. For being a fool. For being a coward. For being *me*, Charles Ryder.

At a guess, this stage is a hurdle to be passed in any acceptance of major incapacity. The railing against fate. The boiling anger at being less than whole. I think some men – some women – never quite clear that hurdle, and become bitter and difficult to live with.

I was helped by Tony, the physiotherapist. A Cornishman with an accent as thick as cream, he was quietly, smilingly derisive of my impatience.

'You're a group-creature, Charles. We all are. In the old days – before history – we lived in caves and hunted in packs. Groups, see? The group was "it". The basic unit. Any part of the group became ill, or old, or lame – anything – that part was left to fend for itself. Left for the predators. Wasn't allowed to endanger the group, see? Part of us – some instinct – remembers this. We all have it. Some more than others, but it's always there. And we try to pretend we *aren't* ill, or old, or lame. I reckon we're still scared of those old prehistoric monsters. Sabre-toothed tigers and the like. That's part of my job, see? To get things working, and to convince people those old sabre-tooths aren't around any more. They're not going to be left. To accept civilisation, see? To accept it deep down inside. It's a real old job, sometimes.'

Maybe there was truth in his theory. Maybe it was a subtle con, aimed at getting me into a better frame of mind. It matters not, because it gradually did the trick. His talk soothed me, as his fingers loosened my muscles and relieved pain. That crazy thing, common to all amputees, the 'ghost limb' gave me trouble. The hand that wasn't there – the hand that had been blown to hell when the Uzi had exploded – was in cramp often during those first few weeks. It would come on in the night, awaken me and force me to flex fingers I no longer possessed.

It scared me at first. Until Tony explained.

'The old body won't yet accept it, Charles. Not yet . . . but in time. What is it? – forty-odd years? – the old nerves have linked the hand and arm to the brain. The brain hasn't had to consciously *think*, see? Just pick up the old pint. Bend the old elbow. Nothing to it. And now it can't, and doesn't know why.' As he talked he massaged the stump, and the cramp gradually eased. 'Like holding the hand and arm in the same position for days on end, see? That's what the nerves tell the brain, and the old brain says, "That should be painful," and kids you on a bit.'

At times it was *very* painful kidding.

Nor was the amputated arm my only problem during that prolonged hospital stay. Twice, I was on the operating table, while they eased ribs and bits and pieces of my side into a more normal position.

The Etonian twit visited me a couple, or three, times. He brought more paperbacks, talked as if we were life-long

170

buddies and hinted that I should make up my mind which corner of the globe I yearned to call 'home'. And, okay, I jollied him along. I'd had a physical hammering, and I was recuperating . . but slowly.

More than that, though. I was gradually changing my mental outlook. Maybe 'growing up'. I wouldn't argue the point. Let's say that as I came to live without an arm I, equally, came to live with myself. As I was, and as I'd always been, and not as I'd *hoped* I was and made believe I was.

The guards. Four of them working a system of eight-hour shifts with, occasionally, a fifth stranger taking a turn. But by and large, four of them. Let's call them Eeny, Meeny, Miny and Mo. We grew to know each other, even to like each other – I certainly knew their first names – and that's why we'll call them Eeny, Meeny, Miny and Mo. Sure, they were guarding me, but as had been pointed out, there was a subtle question. Were they keeping strangers out or were they keeping me *in*?

They didn't intrude. I had complete freedom of the hospital and, later, the hospital grounds. But they were always somewhere around, or standing on the other side of a door, and I had pyjamas and dressing-gown and a pair of slippers. All my other clothes had been taken away and, when I tentatively questioned Tony or the nurses nobody seemed to either know or be prepared to tell me where they were.

But that was okay. For the time being. I was due an artificial arm and, when that was in place and working properly, I'd worked out what I intended to do. All the details. All the risks. Everything.

The guy from the insurance said, 'You should be free of money worries for the rest of your life.'

'That's what they all say.'

He looked puzzled, but didn't ask for an explanation. I stared out of the ward window and watched the mid-August sunshine shimmer the tarmac of the car park. This was the first stage of my plan. The one date I couldn't fix. Great . . . it was here. From now on, I decided things.

'We'll need your signature, Mr Ryder.' He spoke to the back of my neck.

'Sure.'

'I mean a specimen signature. We've opened an account with the money at the Haggthorpe branch of Williams and Glyn's. They'll send a cheque book to you.'

'Not all of it.' I turned and faced him. I gave him a name, and the address of a semi in Kirkby. I said, 'He's dead, but he's left an only child. A daughter. An orphan. Last I heard, she was living with her aunt. Alison, that's her name. Trace her. Half goes to her.'

'Is she expecting it?' He looked slightly worried.

'No, but she's *getting* it.'

'I think you should take time to consider . . .'

'I've "considered",' I interrupted. I smiled a tight, no-nonsense smile. 'It's a decision I won't change. Don't tell her where it came from. Or why. Just drop it in her lap and leave.'

'If you're sure.'

'You can have it in black and white.'

'It – er – it might be better.'

I waved the only hand I possessed, and he sat on the edge of the bed, used his document case as a surface and wrote out the necessary authorisation. He used good paper and he had a good pen. Broad nibbed and able to give character to the writing. It was something I'd almost forgotten. What fine handwriting looked like.

He looked up and said, 'If you care to read it.'

'I trust you.' I was back to staring out of the window.

He sighed. He was up against something not in the book of rules.

172

'If you'll sign it, please,' he said. 'Then I'll witness the signature. Then the specimen signature for the bank.'

'No come-back,' I assured him.

I signed. An awkward signature, and not at all like my usual quick scrawl. Something else I hadn't realised. A new 'autograph'. Not that it mattered too much . . . not if things went smoothly.

At first they went smoothly enough.

By the first day of September (it was a Wednesday) I'd received notification from the Williams and Glyn's bank, along with a cheque book. I was a comparatively rich man. I could afford a good solicitor and, if necessary, a good barrister.

That I could *afford* was enough at this time. I didn't want to show my hand before it was necessary. Which meant before I was safe.

I'd composed the letter. I'd worded it and re-worded it until I was satisfied, then I'd carefully printed it out in block capitals. Not because I wished to disguise my handwriting, but because my left-handed fist was still near-illegible, and I didn't want mistakes. I'd chosen phrases which were deliberately vague; phrases which couldn't be produced in court and held to be oblique admissions of guilt. 'Since our last meeting'. 'I understand you are anxious to meet me'. That sort of thing. I'd addressed the envelope, and now I took it with me when I visited Tony for another session with the artificial arm.

As he adjusted the harness, I said, 'The man outside my door. The man who watches over me – any of them – what do you know about them?'

'I don't ask.' He sounded embarrassed.

'You don't want to know?'

'Orders from administration, see? They're there to look after you. No questions.'

'Those are your instructions?'

'From administration,' he repeated. Then, 'Is it chaffing at all?'

'A little.'

'Where? There?' He touched a part of the stump.

'That's about it.' Then, as he inspected the artificial limb, 'Look, Tony, I want a letter posted.'

'There's a post box near the porter's office.' He kept his eyes fixed on the leather of the arm.

'I know that. I don't want to use it.'

'Charles . . . we've had orders.'

' "We"?'

'Everybody. From up top, see?'

'You think I'm some sort of a criminal?' I asked quietly.

'No, boy. *No*!' He looked up, and there was genuine surprise on his face. 'Some sort of hero, more like. That's what they say.'

' "They"?' I probed.

'People talk,' he muttered. 'Bound to. They reckon you're some sort of special policeman, like. Y'know . . . special.'

'But not to ask?'

'Them's the orders. Strict orders.'

'Okay.' I nodded, slowly. 'You haven't asked. But that much you've guessed. Some sort of "special policeman".'

'I don't want to know, Charles.' He frowned his worry. 'I don't want to lose my job, see? You wouldn't want me to . . .'

'The letter's to another policeman.'

'Oh!'

'It's addressed to his office. You can check the envelope if you like.'

'You can post it in the . . .'

'A friend,' I lied gently. 'Somebody who'll be wondering where I am. Who'll be worried.'

'If it's to another . . .'

'Check it.' I reached towards the dressing-gown which

was draped across the back of a nearby chair. I slipped the enveloped letter from the pocket, and held it out. 'Nothing funny. Nothing underhand.'

'In that case, why not . . .' He scowled at the address. 'Why can't you post it at the hospital box?'

'I can't tell you that, Tony.' It was a good and ready-made ploy. Why should I lie, when I had somebody else's lies at my disposal? I added, 'If I tell you *that*, you'll know more than you should know. More than you might have guessed.'

'The men guarding you?'

It was a weak, last defence. He made no move to return the letter to me.

I smiled at him, and said, 'They know what *you* know. What you've *guessed*. Somebody has to be trusted a fraction farther. Them? Okay, I'm maybe doing them an injustice . . . but I don't *know* them. Only as names. Only as men doing a job. I have to trust *somebody*. I have to make a choice.'

'And – er – y'know, I'm the choice?'

I nodded and knew I'd won.

Saturday, September the 4th, at 2 pm. It wasn't a long shot. It was a very deliberately calculated plan. The postage had been first class, therefore Smith should have received the letter on the Thursday. Certainly no later then Friday. 2 pm gave him time to travel from Haggthorpe, and Saturday visiting hours started at that o'clock. I was waiting and watching, on a path between the car park and the main entrance.

The guard on duty was perhaps twenty yards away. Doing his job, I suppose, but by this time that job had developed into what must have long become a very routine and even boring spell of duty. I'd behaved myself. Never put a foot wrong. Sometimes strolled alone, either along the corridors or out in the hospital grounds. Sometimes passed the time of day with strangers, but never more than that. Other than the Etonian, I hadn't had visitors. Therefore, this Saturday was in no way different, and the guard had no reason for suspicion.

Smith almost walked past me, but I spoke his name. He stopped and for a moment stared.

'You've grown a beard.'

'Just keep chatting,' I said amiably. 'I've no intention of running away.'

'Why the hell should you . . .'

'Keep walking. Talking. We're being watched'. I sauntered along the path, and Smith fell into step alongside me. I allowed him time to grasp the situation, then murmured, 'Into the hospital. Follow the signs to the cafeteria. We'll sit at a table. You can buy me a cup of tea.'

'Look, what the devil . . .'

'Keep it quiet,' I warned. I smiled, as if he'd made some mildly humorous remark. 'Don't turn it into a pantomime. I'm being guarded.'

'*Guarded*!'

'Keep it cool, Smith. You'll have your pound of flesh. You won't even have to work for it.'

'Ryder, I want to know . . .'

'You'll be *told*.' I nodded, as if in agreement with some remark he'd made. I noticed the guard moving in, behind us, but too far away to hear anything. I moved my shoulder in a one-sided shrug, and muttered, 'Keep the con moving, friend. Until we sit at a table.'

'Look, I don't see why the hell . . .'

'As a personal favour.'

'If this was a mental hospital . . .'

'It isn't.'

'. . . I'd think you were crazy.'

'Okay. Humour me.'

I'd kept my artificial hand in the pocket of my dressing-gown. He obviously noticed something odd about my movements.

He asked, 'Have you injured your arm?'

'Something of an under-statement.'

'What?'

'It's been amputated. It isn't there any more.'

'Oh!'

It stopped him, and we walked in silence along the corridors and into the cafeteria. There was an empty table, with space enough around for privacy. I chose it, and Smith peeled off and walked to the counter. He joined me at the table, brought two cups of badly made tea, then sat down and spooned sugar into his drink.

I checked that the guard hadn't entered the room, then in a soft voice, said, 'The last time, you'd arrested me for having shot my wife.'

'To question you.'

'I was *arrested*, friend. You were damn sure.'

'To *question* you,' he repeated. 'And, as I recall, you butted me in the face.'

'Then escaped from custody.'

'You were never *in* custody.' He tasted the tea, and pulled a face. 'Your kids said you and your wife weren't on the best of terms, so . . .'

'So you jumped to the conclusion that *I'd* killed her?'

'The hell I did! What sort of a . . .'

'The hell you *didn't*,' I rasped.

'Why should I do a thing like that?' He matched tone for tone.

'Why do you people do anything?'

'Damn it, man, we may play a little rough sometimes, but we don't invent murders.'

'No?' My lip curled.

'I saw her this morning – to tell her I was coming here – and she . . .'

'You . . .' Something in my expression stopped him in mid-sentence. 'What the hell sort of a trick is this, Smith?'

'She wants to see you.'

'She . . .' I gaped, then breathed, '*She's not dead?*'

'Dead?' This time, he stared.

'You accused me of murdering her.'

'The hell I did. Somebody had shot her. She was in hospital less than a week, but she couldn't be seen for twenty-four hours. We pulled you in for questioning. What sort of bloody . . .'

'*You accused me of murdering her!*' It was a soft shout, but loud enough to attract some small attention.

'Now *you* cool it, Ryder.' He was hanging on to his composure. In fairness, one of us had to. At that moment I was sure one of us was crazy. In a quiet, hard tone, he said, 'She's fitter than you are, and younger than both of us. She was shot. Shot in the side. We didn't know it at the time – we hadn't had chance to interview her – but she'd interrupted some bastard who'd been helping himself to whatever he could find in the house. He lost his nerve, shot her and she flaked out. Shock, loss of blood . . . the usual. The kids talked about a family row, so you had to be seen. That's all . . .'

'That's not all.' The words almost choked me. 'That's not all, Smith. Not by a moon's journey.'

'All right. The men who picked you up played rough. But so did you. We decided to call it tit-for-tat. Give a thumping, take a thumping.'

'Smith, you don't know the half of it. Not a tenth.'

'The man who did the shooting. Early twenties. You don't know him, but he has a conscience – if these animals ever have such a thing – he thought he might have killed her. He gave himself up, two days later, in Huddersfield.'

'Christ Almighty!'

'Since then, you've been listed "Missing From Home". That's why I contacted your wife this morning. She wants to see you.'

'If you're telling the truth . . .'

'Why the hell should I . . .'

'. . . why isn't she with you?'

'Ryder, you're well past the age of discretion. If you want to leave your wife, that's a civil matter. Damn all to do with the police. We check you're okay, then let her know. I talked to her, but that's all. She knows about this visit . . . but not where.'

I believed him. Eventually. Why not? Why should I *not* have believed him. It fitted in, all too neatly. I'd been on the run all this time, and nobody had caught me. Nobody had caught me, because nobody had been *chasing* me.

Judas Christ!

I'd agreed to see Anne. Sure, I'd agreed to see her. Again, why not? I'd lived all this time with the belief that she was dead; that she'd been murdered, and that I was the chief suspect. All this time. All this agony. All this doubling about and back-tracking. All this misery and hole-in-the-corner living.

And now *I* was on somebody's damn 'hit list'.

That night I slept not at all. Nor wanted to. For a year – indeed for rather more than a year – I'd lived an animal existence. I'd lived rough, I'd lived smooth, I'd changed my appearance, I'd changed my personality. You name it, *I'd* done it.

That, not counting the loss of a limb. Not counting the internal hammering. Not counting the present position, where I was required to leave the country and take on a completely new identity. People had died. Tiny had died . . . and others who'd been caught in that ambush. Come to that, *I'd* 'died'. In some subtle way. I certainly wasn't the same Charles Ryder I'd been when I'd walked from Leeds Town Hall, much less the same Charles Ryder who'd been chief clerk at the Haggthorpe branch of Nat West.

Christ, those were the days. Those had *been* the days.

Or had they?

Like a boy wearing his first long trousers. Like a youth tasting his first genuine kiss.

Never the same, friend. Never *ever* the same. The clock goes but one way. The earth has a single, fixed direction of spin. That one, final impossibility; tomorrow can never be yesterday, and this year can never be last year.

Sure, everybody knows that, but so few people fully *realise* it. So few people *appreciate* it.

I did . . . and still do.

It brought heartbreak, but at the same time it brought tranquility. In some strange, back-to-front way, it scared the hell out of me but, equally, it removed all deep-rooted terror. Nothing mattered any more. Nothing was important, nothing could be changed and all the tears and all the heartbreak in the world added up to one big ball of wasted emotion.

On a personal level, the arm would *not* come back, Tiny would *stay* dead and, whatever I'd become would continue to be *me*.

So simple. So basic. But to accept that truth robbed me of sleep.

Anne had worn well. She looked no older than when I'd seen her last. In fact, she looked happier; more content and, to that extent, perhaps a little less haggard, therefore perhaps a little younger. She looked as smart and as trim as ever and, had I not known her for what she was, I might have considered her a fine woman and a wife to be proud of.

I'd more than half-expected her to bring either Tim or Judy, but she came alone and, as she approached me from the car park, I sensed a feeling of preparedness. If I was ready for a fight, she was willing to give me a fight. She didn't *want* it . . . but she was ready.

I didn't want to fight. I didn't want to fight ever again.

I noticed her stiffen slightly, as we came near enough to touch and, although I had no intention of giving her even a

180

token kiss, I guessed that she was preparing herself to turn her face away. I held out my hand, and she almost sighed as she took it in hers.

'The beard suits you.' The tight smile that came and went meant nothing.

I grunted.

'I'm sorry about the arm.'

'Don't be.'

I turned, and we walked side by side towards the hospital. I felt nothing. No love, no hatred . . . nothing. She was a good-looking woman, but even the thought that she'd given life to my own children didn't cross my mind. She was merely one more good-looking woman.

The guard was still there. Too distant to hear us, but near enough for me to see the look of perplexity on his face. Nor did *that* matter. Nor did *anything* matter.

I wasn't bitter. I wasn't angry. I wasn't sad. I was *nothing*.

At the cafeteria she helped me carry tea and chocolate biscuits to an empty table, then she lighted a cigarette and waited.

I tasted the tea, then said, 'Smith passed the message. You wanted to see me.'

'A divorce,' she said softly.

'I almost guessed it.'

'Well?'

'You to divorce me, or me to divorce you?'

'Couldn't it be mutual? A simple break-down?'

'Is it?'

I wasn't being awkward or difficult. I was curious.

'Isn't it?' She gently threw the challenge back at me.

'What would the kids say?'

'Tim's left home.' The cigarette moved more quickly than before to and from her lips. 'He's found work. Shares a flat with a friend.'

'Male or female?'

'One of his pals. A youth about his own age.'

'Very puritanical, our son.' I smiled. 'What about Judy?'

'She'd be happy.'

'Without a father?'

'With . . .' She had the grace to glance away for a moment. 'With a step-father.'

'Nice.' I nodded. Maybe – just maybe – there was an edge to the single word.

'Look, you walked out on me, you left me, and . . .'

'That's the way you see it?'

'What other way? I mean, when a husband goes missing for . . .'

'You can have your divorce,' I interrupted. 'Mutual, one-sided, any way you like. Grab another man while you have looks, but don't say – don't ever *dare* say – I walked out on you.' I waved her silent, then continued, 'No recriminations. Just for the record, and between us two. Then I leave this table and walk out of your life.

'I was no part of a bank robbery. That's so long since, it's almost forgotten . . . but that was the trigger. Despite the verdict, you refused to believe. The kids refused to believe. Smith refused to believe . . . but Smith I can understand. That day when I walked into the bungalow. Twelve strangers had believed me. That, in effect. Twelve strangers, who knew nothing about me. Who'd never met or seen me before. They believed . . . but you didn't. Tim didn't. Judy didn't.

'The bank. Masters. Oh, sure . . . officially, they *couldn't*. Officially, they couldn't believe. At least, not openly. But they could. Masters, see? It depended on him. The manager. If he'd recommended. They'd have taken notice. I know enough about the banking set-up. If Masters had recommended . . .'

I stopped and smiled. That part wasn't important, and she wasn't really interested. She'd never been interested when I'd worked at the bank . . . why the hell should she be interested now?

Why should I even want her to be interested? Could be, I owed her the truth, but I didn't owe her an explanation, much less an excuse.

I chewed some chocolate biscuit, swallowed, tasted my tea, then continued, 'Had you believed. Had you even pretended to believe. Just a pretence, if that's as far as you could go . . . that's all that was necessary. You refused. More than that, even. You refused to allow Tim and Judy to believe. You're a very dominating, very stubborn woman. You always set the pace, always will. You told the kids – impressed your opinion on the kids – and, maybe unknowingly, they both did what you wanted them to do. Rejection, all round. Their father was a criminal. It's what you wanted them to believe . . . the hell with what that belief might do to their lives.

'Let me tell you something . . .' I sipped at the tea. 'I thought they were after me for wife-murder. Smith will have told you. I've been haring from one bolt-hole to the next for more than a year. Not because I gave a damn about you. Dead or alive, I didn't care. Just that I'd ducked one false charge, and I was scared of a second. Scared of something that wasn't even there.

'One more thing, before I leave you . . .' Again, I sipped my tea. Maybe I was getting a little nervy. I think not – I think I'd passed that stage – but who can be sure? 'The thing that separates us from all other living things. You. Me. Every other human being on earth. The thing that makes us unique. Not intelligence. Not a conscience. Not that we can communicate. Can exchange information, record knowledge, build future generations upon past generations. None of these things. We're different – we're unique: because we know death.'

I paused, to let it sink in, then added, 'Something I've learned during the past year. Not to kid myself. To accept it and not choke on it. I'm not immortal. To accept it, and live with it. To *accept* it . . . not just to mouth it. The price of being able to think, see? Of knowing what terror is. Of being crap-scared, because this just *might* be the day. The moment. The sum total of all that's gone before. What everything adds up to.' Again I paused. 'Sit on it, Anne. Lay awake nights, sweating about it. About what it's going to be like. Rough. Smooth. Easy. Hard. It has to be one of them . . . and one day you'll know.' I sighed and drank what was left of my tea. 'That's the gift you gave me. I don't thank you, because it's not a nice gift. So I'm returning it. Sharing it.' I stood up, slowly and smiled down at her. 'Study it,' I ended. 'Know that from every angle it's black. Hopeless. Know that's why I left you. Why Tim's left you. Why Judy will leave you. Go ahead, divorce me. Marry this other guy. But never forget – *never* forget – it won't make a scrap of difference. You'll be alone. On the one day – at the one moment – you really need somebody . . . no way! You go through *that* door solo.'

To scare her? To give her a few sleepless nights? To make damn sure the next time she was ill – *every* time she was ill – she'd sweat a few more cobs and suffer a few more nightmares?

I wouldn't argue. I owed that lady something and saw no reason – *still* see no reason – why some of it shouldn't be repaid. Figuratively speaking, she'd torn a year from my life and turned it into the worst year of my life. Far and away the worst. More that that . . . a year that shouldn't have happened. A year I hadn't deserved.

Therefore, I would not argue. Nor do I apologise.

The bitch deserved no less.

Which was okay by me, but it brought the Etonian out in something of a rash. He was there on the Monday. Mo (let's call him Mo, for the sake of argument) had obviously reported my female visitor. A nice guy, Mo. Very efficient.

He didn't know it, but I intended to drop him . . . but good!

Meanwhile the Etonian lounged elegantly in the armchair and drawled, 'First we've heard of a wife, old man.'

'We don't all flaunt them.'

'Nevertheless, it could have been *anybody*.'

'It was my wife.'

'Women have been known to carry guns.'

'True.'

'And be prepared to use them. They aren't all hit *men*.'

'If I'm going abroad . . .' It was still something of a struggle to fill and light my pipe, one-handed. The dummy hand was of little use in the operation, so I had to concentrate. I began again. 'If I'm going abroad, my wife should know. She might want to go with me.'

'You're making difficulties, Charles.'

'She's deciding. She'll let me know.'

'We might have to move you, for safety's sake.'

'Short of fixing me up – locking me away – putting me in permanent solitary confinement . . .' I put the pipe between my teeth and worked to free a match from the box.

'What?'

'I'll contact her again.'

I managed a match, struck it into flame and clowned around lighting and tamping the tobacco, with one hand.

He said, 'Charles, old boy, why don't you behave yourself?'

'I'm a good boy.' I spoke around the pipe. 'I've decided. Australia.'

'Australia?' He sounded both pleased and interested.

'Can do?'

'But of course.'

'Complete with wife?'

'The impossible takes a little longer.' He smiled his delight, then asked, 'Does she know?'

'Not where. Not yet.'

'You'll tell her, of course.'

'In a fortnight.' I took the pipe from my mouth, and blew smoke. 'I gave her a fortnight to decide. A week next Saturday – if she says "Yes" – I'll tell her, Australia. If she says "No", she won't be told.'

'Not such big difficulties, after all.' The smile broadened a little. 'I'll meet her, of course.'

'A week next Saturday.'

'Fine. I'm looking forward to it.'

'Yeah, I'm sure she is, too.'

He tried to ease her address from me, but I remained obstinately coy. I worked to make it sound like a good argument.

'Leave her for the moment. Till she decides. Then if she says "Yes", you can vet her as much as you like. If she says "No" . . . don't let's add to the little she already knows.'

What might be called 'Giving the Opposition a False Sense of Security'. A change of plan, but basically the *same* plan. Just a little easing here and a little trimming there. The same end, but a different means. A means I had more control over.

To rid myself of it all. To draw a dividing line, beyond which nobody could step, without my permission. Not Anne, not Tim, not Judy. Not Smith, not the Etonian, not emissaries of 'the Colonel'. A land, and a life, in which I might enjoy something of a novelty. At least a novelty for me. A life and what was left of *my* life, without worry, without fear, without pressure and without manipulation. Such a novelty . . . but I was determined to claim it.

Which is why at a few minutes before time started nibbling its way through Wednesday, September the 15th, I was belting Mo across the side of the skull and realising that black-jacking a grown man into unconsciousness wasn't as easy as the general run of blood-and-guts books would have

186

you believe. He was going under, but he was going under slowly and with something of a struggle and, sure as hell, I didn't want to kill him. I heeled the door of the ward closed, thought about smacking him with the edge of the chair, then had second thoughts and bent down to check what he was groping for.

The shoulder-holster . . . what else? The Beretta Modello 1934. A real 'James Bond' handgun, and one-and-a-half pounds of machined steel. That was great, and just what I needed. I dragged it from the holster, checked that the safety catch was on, then smacked him behind the right ear with the flat surface of the barrel. That did the trick beautifully.

Thereafter, surgical tape.

I took his coat off first, then taped his wrists together. Then a tape across his eyes. Then, off with the trousers and the ankles and knees taped together. He was making snoring noises and obviously coming round, so that meant I could tape the lips together. He was trussed very firmly. The one thing available in a hospital is broad, surgical tape. I had more than enough. I even used it to fasten him to the upright of the radiator . . . by which time he was moving around and, no doubt, wondering what the hell was coming next.

He couldn't see and he couldn't talk. His movements were very restricted. He could only guess, and I left him to do just that.

Meanwhile, and one-handed, I started using the nail scissors. My face over the wash-bowl, and the water running, I removed as many whiskers as possible. It took half an hour, and then I was ready for the shaving foam and the disposable razor. Again, one-handed. Again, with the water running. But I ended up clean-shaven once more, with most of my beard sluiced down the drain. It felt clean. New. A new-born-baby feeling, and I took it as a good omen.

The suit fitted. I knew it would; that's why I'd earmarked Mo. The ignition key was in the hip pocket, and I dropped the Beretta into the pocket of the jacket before I climbed from the window of the ward and soft-footed my way towards the car park and his parked Austin.

I had all I needed. My cheque book, toilet bits and pieces, a semi-automatic pistol and the use of a car for a few hours. I drove carefully. It was surprisingly easy; I steadied the steering wheel with the dummy hand whenever I needed to change gear and the rest was like eating cherries.

Dawn found me where I wanted to be. Back in the Dales. It's a big place and in parts a lonely place, and it's where I am as I end this catalogue of catastrophe. I left the car to be found and walked.

I'm still walking. Not hurrying, just walking. Neither am I running.

I'm searching. Carefully and methodically. Asking a few questions here, putting out a few feelers there. Given time, I'll find them – or they'll find me – the Kelly family. Come Spring, I'll be at Appleby; at the annual Horse Fair, where the travelling people all congregate and tend to run wild.

Tommy, too, at a guess. If only to get drunk and enjoy a fight. I know the man. I know what he is, but I don't yet know *where* he is.

But I'll find him, and when I do . . .

The running has ended. The searching will be ended. Thereafter only peace, and the company of the only people I can still call 'friend'.